FIRE AND BLOOD

FIRE AND BLOOD
A Novel

by William Garlington

Pioneer Paperback Series

Kalimát Press
Los Angeles

Manufactured in the United States of America

Library of Congress Cataloging in Publication Data

Garlington, William, 1947–
  Fire and blood.

  (Pioneer paperback series)
  1. Bahai Faith--History--Fiction. 2. Babism--
History--Fiction. I. Title.
PS3557.A7164F5 1984   813'.54   84-3882
ISBN 0-933770-08-1

To all those who have died for
their heretical beliefs,
past and present.

Chapter 1

THE DOOR OPENED. In walked a young man flanked by military escorts. His brown cloak, opening over a colored under-robe and white linen, was modest yet dignified. The green turban that crossed the middle of his forehead gave him a look of distinction that eclipsed his twenty-nine years. Above his delicate olive cheeks sat piercing brown eyes which dominated the remainder of his neatly bearded face and added a dimension of animated strength to his small stature.

In military gray uniforms and black boots, the guards ushered the man into the large hall filled with ecclesiastical dignitaries. Viewing the scene, they soon realized that the only empty seat was the one reserved for the heir to the Persian throne Crown Prince Násiri'd-Dín. Looking like confused children, they halted suddenly and ordered their prisoner to do the same. The young man, however, did not hesitate. With an expression of overpowering self-confidence, he pulled himself free from the astonished guards and proceeded to seat himself in the royal chair.

Normally such an act would have brought forth an immediate response from the onlookers, but the spirit emanating from the man's being seemed momentarily to stun the mullás. They could only sit and gaze at him in wonder. Even the entry of the Crown Prince, whose place had been usurped, did not break the mysterious silence. Rather than ordering the man to leave the chair, the prince quietly acquiesced by seating himself among the men who had invited him to the hearing.

1

After several minutes, one of the mullás rose to his feet. With a swaying gait that resembled a rickety old cart, he slowly traversed the twenty or so feet that separated the young man from his tribunal. When he was within arm's distance of his destination, the divine stopped. Stroking his full gray beard, he looked menacingly into the face before him. Like his captive, the mullá possessed a look of assurance common among those men who are convinced of the indisputable truth of their position. But while the young man's intensity was balanced by a strange aura of serenity, the mullá's earnestness, depicted by the deep ridges on his brow, knew no restraint.

"We have heard that you make momentous claims," the mullá finally exclaimed, "and it is the wish of His Imperial Majesty that you set forth these claims before the distinguished doctors of our religion, that they might establish the truth or falsity of what you say."

Clearing his throat and turning so that his face was visible to both the examiners and the examined, the mullá resumed his address. "As for myself, I am only a humble servant of God. But holding the highest ecclesiastical position in this city, my conversion would not be without significance. Of greater importance, however, would be the winning to your cause of the Crown Prince, who assures me with his most exalted word that he is ready to follow you if he merely be persuaded that your claims are true. All that you have to do is give us some kind of proof."

The speaker's reference to the Crown Prince, whose black fez, royal-blue military dress jacket, and gold shoulder tassels stood out boldly in the surrounding sea of brown robes, caused a sudden turning of heads among the divines. For a brief moment it seemed that the entire assembly had focused their eyes on the young nobleman. Only the stony brown irises beneath the green turban remained steadfast.

"Now I have several questions to ask you," continued the mullá. "First, the books composed in the style of our Holy Book, the most illustrious Qur'an, which have been disseminated throughout the land in your name—are they your compositions, or do your followers wrongly attribute them to you?"

Without any sign of emotion, the young man responded. "They are from God."

The man's answer produced a buzzing among the brown-robed, black-turbaned divines, causing the mullá to delay his questioning. Patiently he waited for the noise to subside. When the murmurs were all but gone, he once again pursued his course. "But you have penned them?"

"Yes."

"You mean to say then, that you are like the Tree on Sinai?" asked the amazed mullá.

"Mercy be upon you," replied the man, again withholding from his countenance any indication of emotion.

A look of exaggerated astonishment crossed the mullá's face and was quickly copied by his fellow divines. Then, lowering his eyebrows, the black-turbaned inquisitor returned to his examination. "You are called by your followers the Báb. Who gave you this title?"

"God gave me this title."

"When?"

"Before creation."

"And to what does it refer?"

"To the Gate of the City of Knowledge."

"Then you are the Gate of the City of Knowledge, the Doorway to the Prophet of God?"

"Yes."

"Praise be to God!" shouted the mullá in a voice flowing with sarcasm. "I have waited all my life to meet such a person, and now you have come to my city—even to my

3

very mosque. Just a few signs of proof, and I will be your undying servant."

"What proof do you require?" asked the young man, his eyes darting to meet those of his interrogator.

"Well," droned the mullá, "as the Prophet of God—peace be upon him—hath declared, knowledge is twofold: knowledge of medicine and knowledge of theology. Can you tell me why it is that some cases of indigestion are capable of treatment and others lead to more serious disorders?"

"I am not a doctor of medicine," the young man replied.

The response set off another murmuring buzz among the seated divines, who leaned one way and then another to consult hastily over the strange answer they had just heard. It was finally the Crown Prince who terminated their consultation by rising to his feet. "If it be so that you are the Gate of the City of Knowledge," he yelled, "and yet you say that you have no knowledge of medicine, then this is quite incompatible with your claim."

The young man did not answer him with words. All the prince received was a cold stare.

"Perhaps theology is more to your liking," said the mullá, resuming his questioning and leaving the Crown Prince to seat himself again.

Still the man's lips remained sealed.

Ignoring the silence, the mullá went on. "Theology consists of the sciences of Principles and Applications. The science of Principles has a beginning and a conclusion. Tell me then, are the divine attributes of knowledge, seeing, and power identical with the Divine Essence; or are they separate entities distinct from it?"

"Identical with the Essence."

"Then God is multiple?" The mullá's voice rose noticeably in pitch.

4

"There is only one God," said the man stoically.

"If this be the case," continued the now excited mullá, "your statement shows a great deal of confusion. For your information, young man, the truth is that Divine Essence and Divine Knowledge are two things, like vinegar and syrup, which have yet become identical. God is compounded of the Divine Essence, plus knowledge of the Divine Essence, plus power and other attributes. Moreover, the Divine Essence is without an opposite, but knowledge has an opposite which is ignorance. Besides this, God knows, the Prophet—peace be upon him—knows, and we know. We partake, therefore, in knowledge. We also have a ground for distinction, for the knowledge of God is from Himself, while our knowledge is obviously from Him. Therefore, it is manifestly clear that God is compounded of a ground of distinction and a ground of identity, but He is not identical with His attributes."

The mullá's harangue brought forth gazes of envious admiration from the assembled divines, a recognition he acknowledged by parading himself up and down in front of his victim in the manner of a conquering rooster. His victory strut, however, was suddenly interrupted when the young man calmly and assuredly broke the silence.

"Beware of those things that begin and end with words," he said.

The mullá's lips curled tightly. Stopping in his tracks, this most senior of the divines turned in the direction of his colleagues. After a pause to regain his composure, he snapped back to face the defendant. "Since you have raised the issue of words," he said in a stern but controlled voice, "could you conjugate for us in the language of our Holy Book the verb 'to strike' in all its forms?"

"I am not a grammarian."

After another pause the mullá retorted, "Well, perhaps

you could explain to us the meaning of the following tradition which Muḥammad—peace be upon him—is known to have uttered: 'It is He who maketh you to behold the lightning, a fear and a hope.'"

"You are the scholar."

"But it is you," scowled the mullá, "who claim to be the Gate of the City of Knowledge."

"Not the knowledge of which you speak."

Again the mullá paused, and for several long moments he stared at the prisoner. Then, with a sweeping wave of his hand, he continued. "Please tell us then, O one who is dumb in the realm of words and dumb in the realm of ideas, what virtues do you possess?"

"My verses are inspired by God," the man replied. With this announcement, he abruptly rose to his feet and began to chant in a melodious voice: "Praise be to God who has created the heavens! Glory be to He who has molded the clay."

A sudden shout from the gallery interrupted the man's song. The voice belonged to the Crown Prince, who was now on his feet. "In his very first utterance, he who would claim to be inspired by God has made the most fundamental grammatical error. This any schoolboy could see."

Unlike his first encounter with the nobleman, when the young man in the green turban had virtually ignored the prince, this time he responded with a volley of words. "The Holy Book which you claim to be infallible is not based on the rules and conventions current among men. The glorious Word of God can never be subjected to the limitations of his creatures. Nay, the rules and canons of grammar which men have adopted and so elaborately codified are deduced from the Holy Book, not vice versa."

Having riveted his attention on the Crown Prince, the man was slow to notice the mullá approaching him. When he finally beheld the black apparition, the divine's hand was already swinging in a direct line to the right side of his face. The force of the blow knocked his head back and caused his green turban to tumble to the floor beside him.

"Remember to whom you are speaking," growled the mullá.

The man picked up his turban and deliberately adjusted it to his head. Then, without the least indication of lost dignity, he returned the mullá's comment. "You should follow your own advice."

"And what is that supposed to mean?" asked the mullá in a surprised tone.

"You should respect my station."

"And what is that?"

"I am, I am, I am the promised One! I am the One whose name you have for a thousand years invoked, at whose mention you have risen, whose advent you have longed to witness, and the hour of whose Revelation you have prayed God to hasten. Verily I say, it is incumbent upon the peoples of both the East and the West to obey my word and to pledge allegiance to my person."

"Then you are the Qá'im, the Lord of Religion?" gasped the mullá in a voice that registered both his surprise and mockery.

"Yes," the man said boldly.

Once again the assemblage became alive with activity. As before, divines young and old turned one way and then another to consult with their fellows, the swarm of black turbans resembling a hive of angry bees. "He is crazy," some of them murmured. "Blasphemy!" others cried. In the same manner, the Crown Prince again made himself heard, exchanging virulent, if hasty, remarks with the mullás closest to him.

Suddenly, one of the younger divines rose to his feet.

Gaining the attention of those around him, he addressed the man in the green turban. "I am not tied to words. Show me a miracle that is suitable to your title, and I will certainly become your follower. For example, His Imperial Majesty, the shah, is ill. Restore him to health."

A hush fell over the room as the clerics awaited the man's reply.

"It is not within my power," he answered.

"Then it would seem," grunted the older mullá, "that all you have to offer is illiterate verse."

"My life is my proof," the man shot back.

"Fortunately, I cannot see your life," scoffed the mullá, "for it is probably as unchaste as your verse."

The divines' appreciation of their colleague's wit was evidenced by the numerous chuckles that broke out among them. Some were noticeably vocal in their amusement, but all were unanimous in finding his remark humorous. Even the Crown Prince, who was well known for his somber nature, could not hold back a faint smile.

Like a man who had not been let in on a common joke, the defendant sat unmoved, his eyes fixed on the far wall. But as the laughter began to subside, he rose to his feet and solemnly proclaimed his thoughts. "Far be the glory of thy Lord, the Lord of all greatness, from what they impute to Him, and peace be upon His apostles."

Now, what had only seconds before been a scene of lighthearted jest was transformed into a seething sea of invective. From one side of the outraged assembly to the other, words of scorn filled the air. Everywhere the green turban turned, it was greeted with scowls and glowers. Some mullás raised their hands wildly in the air, while others pounded their fists on the small wooden tables in front of them.

From amid this tumultuous uproar, a spectacled mullá with a flowing black beard sprang up. "You wretched and immature lad," he shouted. "You have already convulsed and subverted much of our land. Recant your heresy!"

Almost immediately the cry of a second divine echoed through the chamber. "Hold your peace, you perverse follower of Satan."

"Your honor," interrupted the man, addressing the chief examiner and quieting the divines with the authority of his voice, "may I remind you that I did not come here of my own accord. It will please you to remember that I was summoned to this city."

"And may I remind you," countered the mullá, "that it was I who ordered you here, and it is I who will determine your fate."

"God is the architect of fate."

"It is I who will determine your fate!" repeated the mullá, slamming his fist down on the wooden railing that separated him from the examinee.

"Do you claim to be God?"

The mullá froze, searching mentally for a way out of his verbal dilemma, while his colleagues grew silent. "Such a Qá'im is worthy of such a God," he said, throwing his hands up in disgust. Turning his back on the sayyid, he waddled back to his seat.

The mullá had planned that his arrival would be a signal to the doorkeeper that the examination was over. The guards were then to usher the prisoner from the hall. However, in the same manner that he had seated himself at the beginning of the hearing, the green-turbaned youth foiled his interrogator's plans by rising to his feet, standing down from the royal chair, and boldly making his way unescorted toward the large wooden doors. Thus, by the time the mullá was in his seat and had begun to put his plan into action, the young man was only a few feet away from his destination. Too late to object, the mullá could only look on in frustration at the man's audacity, and the equally amazed doorkeeper found himself automatically swinging open the huge portals and allowing the sayyid to depart the room unhindered.

THE NEXT MORNING, the young man was again summoned to the ecclesiastical court. This time, instead of being brought before the religious doctors, he found himself escorted down a narrow passageway that ended at a heavily bolted wooden door. Behind the barrier was a bare-walled, scant-spaced room, without furniture except for a wooden bench in the middle of the floor. Turning the lock, the guard swung open the door and allowed his charge to enter. No sooner had the man crossed the threshold than the door was bolted shut.

Alone, the young sayyid seated himself on the bench and stared pensively at the brown wall in front of him. A few rays of sunlight entering from the lone, barred window atop the adjacent wall gave the room its only illumination. Although the man had no observers, he still maintained an air of reverent dignity. Meticulously folded hands, erect posture, and unmoving brow evinced an inner certitude, while the delicate smile which remained on his face bespoke unfathomable repose.

The road that had brought him here was short but steep. Even as a child he had been different. Working long hours in the family cloth shop, he had marvelled at the constant haggling over inanimate material; while at school he had frustrated his teachers with his disregard for their knowledge. Only when he traveled to the Holy Shrines in Karbala was he happy. He would spend hours on end in those sanctuaries reveling in the ecstasy of devotion.

He continued on this path, spending time with the famed Sayyid Kázim, whose teachings foretold the imminent appearance of the Lord of the Age. With unrestrained passion he had prayed for His coming. Then, in spiritual convulsion one spring night, he had realized that he himself was the chosen one. From there, he had gathered his first eighteen disciples and made his pilgrimage to Mecca. There he publicly proclaimed his mission and initiated the wrath of the authorities that was to follow—an indignation which was to drive him from his native city of Shiraz and result in his eventual arrest and incarceration in a remote mountain fortress far to the north. Having twice been summoned by the ecclesiastical court of Tabriz, he awaited his fate in silence.

He did not have to wait long. The sound of a moving latch announced a visitor. Turning his head, he was confronted by the figure of Mullá Mámáqání, scroll in hand. The divine, whose black turban was matched in its stygian hue by his bushy eyebrows and cold eyes, hesitated momentarily and then addressed the man in a tone similar to the one he had adopted during the course of the previous day's examination. "The court has come to its decision."

Slowly raising the document to eye level, so as to take advantage of the light streaming into the room from the empty passageway behind him, the mullá began to read aloud. "The Royal Ecclesiastical Court of Tabriz finds that Mírzá 'Alí-Muḥammad, otherwise known as Sayyid-i Báb, is of unsound mind. Upon the application of the bastinado he is to be returned to his prison in the northern provinces and kept under close surveillance. In the future should any doubt as to his mental condition be removed, or should he continue to persist in spreading his seditious doctrines, the sentence of an incorrigible apostate will without hesitation be executed upon him.''

Lowering the scroll and purposefully rolling together its ends with his vein-studded hands, the mullá glanced down at the man, who remained perfectly still. As their eyes met, a look of interminable contempt came over the mullá's face. For several seconds he remained unmoved, his anger seemingly carved into stone. Then, turning as if to leave, he took one step toward the door before an afterthought caused him to face the green turban once again. Contorting his lips, he cleared his throat and showered the young man's brow with a spray of yellow saliva. His gesture complete, he left the room, slamming the door behind him.

Chapter 2

A STOLID SUN BEAT DOWN, robbing the parched land of any remnant of moisture. In the distance a lone, turbaned rider, drained of energy and longing for relief, urged his tired horse forward. Now and again brief gusts of wind arose, but they only added dust to the incubated atmosphere. Sun, heat, dust—changeless, monotonous. Tufts of wild grass, sagebrush, the odd tree all became dwarfed into insignificance by the fiery, yellow sphere.

The rider, a gray-robed man in his mid-twenties named Hasan-i Bastami, tried to forget his current predicament by focusing his thoughts on the future. How would he tell his brother Nematullah the news? And, how would the new head of the family react? His father might have understood, but death had taken him. Nematullah was different —stubborn and uncompromising.

A gust of wind swirled dust and sand at the feet of the dapple gray Arab, causing the steed to pull away violently to one side. Only Hasan's strong arms righted the animal's course.

Having calmed his horse, his thoughts returned. Perhaps he should keep quiet. The next few days would be filled with activity, and he could inform Nematullah later—in a letter? No, he knew this was impossible. He had postponed telling him for over a month now and could no longer keep the truth hidden. Even if it meant the unpleasantness of listening to one of Nematullah's diatribes, he had to do what was right.

By now the beads of sweat which had gathered on Hasan's forehead and cheeks had formed small rivulets and begun to trickle into his dark, bushy eyebrows and two-day-old stubble. In a like manner, drops of moisture dripped from his handsomely narrow, if slightly hooked, nose onto the bristles of his well-kept mustache. Swivelling around to have more freedom, he reached down into his bulging saddlebags and pulled out a rough brown cloth with which he wiped the perspiration from his sunburned face. He crumpled the damp cloth, shoved it into a pocket of his robe, and softly murmured to his mount. "Just a little further."

Another thirty minutes passed before the weary rider saw a slight dip in the road, and on the horizon a clump of trees—the signs of the oasis and the caravanserai. As he drew closer, Hasan could see the gleam of the blue tiles on the dome of a small mosque. Soon the caravanserai itself was visible. His goal now in sight, he urged his horse on with a series of quick thrusts to the animal's flanks. Sensing the shade and refreshment of the stable, the steed bolted. Minutes later, they were passing under the compound's gateway.

Their entrance was announced by the rapid clatter of the Arab's hooves on stone. Starting at the gate, the paved pathway passed beside the mosque before veering left around the lodge to terminate at the stables near the rear of the compound. On either side of the roadway stood thin cedar trees, interspersed with a number of pomegranate bushes, whose fallen leaves formed a flowing carpet of yellow. Below the mosque lay an unkempt garden, while beyond the towering trees on the right stood a clear pond whose spring-blue water was the reason for the existence of the solidly constructed, white-walled guest quarters situated behind.

As they passed the mosque, Hasan noticed that a number of tiles had fallen from the structure's dome, and it crossed his mind that the building was in need of repair. Once a center of local pilgrimage, the house of worship now seemed virtually abandoned. Indeed, it was rare to find any believers at all inside. Even the guests of the caravanserai, who once flocked to its inner sanctum, now rarely paid a visit. Perhaps because there was no longer a residing mullá, the last one having left over a year ago to manage the affairs of a newly dedicated mosque five miles away. Or possibly, as Nematullah claimed, travelers these days were more interested in the balance of their account books than in long Arabic sermons.

Once the mosque was behind them, there remained only two hundred yards to the stables, and it was hardly any time at all before both horse and rider were refreshing themselves with draughts of clear, cool water.

His thirst quenched, Hasan left his animal in the care of the stable hands, and Aziz, the master of the stable, led him to the entrance of a large garden. Winding his way past the few scrawny rose bushes that lined the lodge, Hasan approached the doors of the house. His brother's servant 'Abdu'l-Rahim had seen him approaching from the roof and rushed downstairs. "Welcome, master. Peace be upon you. I pray God has blessed your trip," he said.

"A tiring, but safe journey." Hasan followed the man into the house.

"Praise be to God that you are in time for tomorrow's festivities. We feared you might arrive too late."

"Is Nematullah Khán here?"

"He should just be rising from his afternoon nap," answered 'Abdu'l-Rahim as he brought a tray of ripe fruit to the table. The servants will inform him that you have arrived." He withdrew reverently.

Hasan seated himself on a divan. The fruit 'Abdu'l-Rahim had offered him, a selection of melons carved into a variety of shapes and sizes, looked inviting. But the anticipation of meeting his brother left the young man without an appetite.

The anteroom's decorations indicated its owner was a man of good taste. Across the floor were spread finely woven rugs, four in number, on whose milky-white backgrounds sat bold maroon figures that both accentuated and complimented the hues of the room's three large divans. Between these masterpieces of the weaver's craft sat a huge wooden table, its legs covered with delicately carved animal figures, and its top inlaid with tiny pieces of brass fastidiously arranged in a geometric pattern. Scattered throughout the room were a number of smaller tables, all of which supported a variety of objects, including brass ornaments and exquisite miniature paintings.

Hasan played nervously with his hands, as he thought with loathing of the festivities to which 'Abdu'l-Rahim had alluded. As district tax collector, Nematullah was being honored by a royal visit. To Nematullah the visit, with all its pomp and ceremony, was an occasion for extreme pride. But to his younger brother, it was more of a curse.

Sounds of movement in the hallway brought a sudden halt to Hasan's daydreaming. Looking up, he rose to his feet and watched his brother come into the room. A large, well-groomed man, Nematullah wore a spotless brown cloak which opened in the front over a cream tunic. Only a few streaks of gray in his hair and beard revealed his age as over forty. His skin, pampered by precious oils, might have belonged to a man fifteen years younger. Although slightly overweight, he carried himself as if accustomed to athletic endeavor.

Nematullah reached the bottom step and opened his arms. Seconds later the brothers were embracing, placing the ritualistic kiss on each other's cheeks, and exchanging formal greetings. "And how is mother?" said Nematullah, finally pulling away.

"As well as can be expected," replied Hasan. "She still spends a great deal of time thinking about father, but her brother has been extremely kind to all of us. And Tehran's climate seems to agree with her."

"And Amin?"

Hasan swallowed hard and answered as calmly as he could. "He has gone to the east."

Nematullah hesitated. The look on his face seemed to indicate that he had not heard properly. Then, almost unable to control himself, he began to bellow. "You mean he has gone to join those fanatics? How could he be taken in by such nonsense? Has he completely lost his sanity?"

Hasan was prepared for such an outburst. "He believes in their cause."

"What you mean, if you bother to examine it," retorted Nematullah, "is that he has been led astray by that madman the authorities have locked up. What I don't understand is why the mullás don't execute him. Sending him off to the mountains will not solve the problem. You must eliminate a cancer at its source or it will continue to spread. As long as he remains alive there will be trouble."

"You may well get your wish. It is rumored that they will soon bring him to trial."

"As far as I am concerned, it won't be soon enough." Nematullah made a gesture of disgust.

"But have you examined what this 'madman' is saying?" Hasan found himself prodding his brother verbally.

"I don't have to examine what he is saying! Any man who claims to receive visions from God or to be the vehicle

17

of divine knowledge, or whatever nonsense he proclaims, is dangerous. There is only one place for such a man, and it isn't in a mountain prison."

"As I recall," said Hasan, trying to remain calm, "the Prophet himself—peace be upon him—made such claims. In principle, there is no difference between the Prophet Muḥammad and this young Sayyid-i Báb. The Báb's claims may well be false, but one cannot deny them out of hand. They must be examined."

"To tell you the truth," responded Nematullah, "I think the Prophet was probably mad. But all that is a matter of history. What concerns me now, and should concern you, is that our younger brother has run off to join a band of religious fanatics!" Throwing his hands up in the air Nematullah paced furiously toward the other end of the room. The blood vessels in his neck were pounding so hard that Hasan could clearly see them rise and fall.

"Such men are unaware of the forces they unleash," he continued impulsively. "In the name of some spiritual call they tear apart the fabric of society. They turn father against son, brother against brother. They sacrifice family and nation for their own selfish ends."

"Perhaps sometimes the fabric needs to be torn."

Nematullah turned sharply and looked at Hasan as only he could. "Listen to yourself," he shouted. "You speak of tearing apart society as if it were a piece of cloth. Society —the nation, the family—is the one thing that keeps men from returning to the state of animals, and you want to tear it up!"

"There are more important things than order and security," Hasan snapped.

"Only a naive youth could say such things," shot back Nematullah. "Perhaps you should see a society that lacks order and security."

For the next few minutes neither brother spoke. After a time, however, the silence began to affect Hasan. In an effort to calm his anxiety, he walked across the room and stopped in front of the open shutter. Staring deliberately into the garden, he waited for the calm to end. Meanwhile, Nematullah maintained his angry but mute posture.

Finally unnerved by the situation, Hasan returned to the battle. "Can't you see, my brother, that Amin feels he has been called by God? And neither you nor any other person, whatever the intention, has the right to stand between a man and his God."

Hasan's volley of words opened the way for Nematullah, who lost no time in countering. "You speak of God with such assurance," he said in a voice brimming with cynicism. "Are you saying that I am to countenance the actions of a man solely because he claims that God has called on him to carry them out? God is a word which any fool can use to mean anything he imagines. How am I to know if it is God or Satan who has called him? Many men have been called by God, and yet today there is not a single trace of them or their divinely inspired messages. Their gods were buried with them."

The break in Nematullah's discourse gave Hasan the opportunity to reply, but the young man was reflecting on his older brother's words. And thus after a brief spell, it was Nematullah who once again spoke. "Don't you understand, Hasan? God is a meaningless term. There is no way the existence of anything of this kind can be verified. You have studied the philosophers. Most of them, at least those who are honest with themselves, admit that belief in God is a matter of faith, not a matter of knowledge. And what is faith? Another word like God! One knows faith through God and God through faith—a fine state of affairs!"

"Men believe in God because of the Prophets," replied

Hasan. "They see in these men signs of divinity that cannot be ignored. Most men are not philosophers; they see and believe."

"Alas! You are finally right," shouted Nematullah as if he had won a victory. "Most men are nothing but idiots."

Nematullah's sarcasm struck deep, and Hasan's initial response was to leave. From a practical point of view this was impossible of course. But he also knew that, whether he liked it or not, Nematullah was now the head of the family and was due some respect. Thus, making every effort to quell his anger, the young man stood his ground and pondered what to say next.

As it turned out, such reflection was unnecessary. Nematullah made a quick turn and, with a beaming smile, motioned to his brother to step forward. "Come," he said, "you have had a long trip, and we are being hasty. After a bath, supper, and a good night's sleep, you will be of clearer mind." Then, turning toward the door, he shouted his orders. "'Abdu'l-Rahim! Prepare the bath for Hasan."

Hasan knew only too well what his brother was doing. This was Nematullah's way of saying that he had heard enough. Although still angry and frustrated, he resigned himself to the fact that Nematullah would not speak about Amin again that day.

"As for me," continued the older brother, "I have work to do in preparation for tomorrow. Fortune has indeed shone its face on us, my dear Hasan." Again reminding 'Abdu'l-Rahim of his duties, he passed through the door and out into the garden.

Chapter 3

"SALAAM ALEIKAM," Nematullah called out as he watched Hasan descend the stairs. "Come and eat; the table is already prepared."

The head of the household had not lied. As Hasan could see, the breakfast spread before him was lavish: mounds of snow-white rice; numerous morsels of roast lamb covered with mint sauce; a giant omelette sprinkled with herbs and onions; long slender slices of Isfahan melon; bowls full of overripe apricots and pears; and three varieties of fruit juice.

I am really not hungry, Hasan wanted to say. But knowing that his refusal would not be accepted, in spite of the large quantity of food he had consumed the night before, he silently seated himself and allowed his plate to be filled.

During the next few minutes, there was no exchange of words as both men ate their breakfast: Nematullah voraciously, Hasan with less enthusiasm. Outside, the sun was well above the horizon, its rays sending streams of light through the open shutters.

"About Amin . . ." Hasan finally found the courage to say.

"Not today," interrupted Nematullah sternly. "A very important event is about to take place—one which will not only bring the family more wealth, but will greatly raise its prestige. I do not want to ruin these thoughts by having to discuss Amin's foolishness with a bunch of rebel heretics—may their fathers burn in hell! We will talk about him at another time."

While Hasan sat quietly, Nematullah paused to take a large bite of herb-laced egg. When he had completely consumed the mouthful, he again looked at his younger brother. "You know, don't you, that we will dine personally with the prince?"

Expecting a joyful response, Nematullah's eyes opened wide. But when Hasan merely peered imperviously out the window, the older brother appeared taken aback. Grasping the young man by the arm, he raised his voice another octave. "Do you know what this means? Such visits are usually restricted to members of the nobility. By coming here the prince is giving our family his blessing."

"And at what cost to the peasantry?" said Hasan finally.

Letting loose Hasan's arm, Nematullah sat back in his chair and wiped the corners of his mouth with the silken serviette he held tightly in his right hand. He had thought that his brother might ask such a question, focusing on the negative aspects of the royal visit rather than its long-term benefits, and his own response was already prepared. "Yes, the peasants will have to tighten their belts a bit this winter, but they have not complained unduly. In fact, they seem honored that the prince would come here and bless this district with his royal presence."

Feeling that this white lie would satisfy his brother's skepticism, Nematullah was now ready to reveal his trump card. Again leaning forward, he filled his round face with a conspiratorial smile. "You see, my dear little brother, there is more to this visit than I have told you. The prince has just been called upon by the shah to take control of the government of this province, and he brings with him a royal edict appointing me to the position of District

Assessor. As of today, not only will I be in charge of collecting revenue, I will determine what it should be. As a result, the family's wealth will surely double."

Once again Hasan's response to his brother's enthusiasm was little more than a pensive glance. "You mean he will give you license to plunder," he mumbled inaudibly.

The fact that Hasan still sat unmoved would have been more than enough ammunition for Nematullah to pursue the conversation even further, but the unexpected arrival of 'Abdu'l-Rahim from the kitchen changed his line of thought. "Excuse me, master," interjected the servant, bowing. "The prince's cooks and tent pitchers have arrived."

Nematullah hoisted himself up and threw the crumpled serviette on the table. "I must leave," he announced, "but relax and enjoy your meal. Tonight you will see that which few are privileged to witness."

THAT AFTERNOON HASAN STOOD atop the roof of the caravanserai and watched as the royal retinue approached. In the garden below, the handiwork of the prince's servants was evident: large billowing tents filled with courtly apparel and matching in color the hue of the red roses surrounding them; marble fountains constructed in the form of fish and bubbling forth their frothy liquids. Draped across the front of the building's exterior wall, flapping gently in the afternoon breeze, was a huge curtain on whose purple silk finish was embroidered the royal emblem. And, as if not to allow visual images to have a complete monopoly on the assault of the senses, from the nearby kitchen the aromas of the finest delicacies wafted skyward.

Between the constructed paraphernalia, winding its way from the entry gate to the foot of the specially constructed dais located in front of the doorway of the largest tent, was a row of gifts his brother would bestow upon his regal visitor: fine Shirazi carpets, exquisite silks from India, elaborate shawls and brocades, and countless rows of colored cloth, the value of which was beyond estimate.

It did not take a man of genius to figure out where these gifts had come from. Hasan well knew that the carpets and silks had been purchased with borrowed funds, for which a special village tithe would be exacted next winter. The remainder of the cloth was a collection of newly spun winter clothing which Nematullah had seen fit to extract from his peasants on threat of higher grain taxes.

As for the imperial train, it was as ornately choreographed as the garden was designed. The procession opened with ornament-headed heralds who carried in their hands the distinguishing club of office and proclaimed the prince's arrival to the peasants and villagers lining the roadway. Behind them were the official carpet spreaders who, by means of long sticks, ensured that the thoroughfare remained clear of any obstacle. Then came rows of well-dressed officers of the stable, carrying on their shoulders endless varieties of equestrian equipment. After them appeared the prince's shoe bearer, his ewer-and-basin bearer, the carrier of his cloak, and the comptroller of his opium box, all attired in the most lavish silk costumes. Immediately in front of the mounted nobleman was another corps of elaborately costumed men, attendants whose black velvet coats were liberally sprinkled with gold coin. As for the royal figure, surrounded by soldiers and bodyguards, he was by comparison rather simply dressed, the only sign of extravagance being the brightly jeweled holt of a bronze-sheathed sword which hung from the side of his military blue uniform. Completing the line were the Master of the Horse and the Court Poet, both of whom were draped in fancy brocade robes and attended by their own corps of servants. In all, about two thousand noblemen and attendants were on display.

While the prince proudly dismounted and the party gathered together in preparation for their official entry, Hasan felt a tightening in his stomach. His mind contrasted the needless exhibition before him with the harsh poverty of the district's rural population. Here was one man wallowing in luxury at the expense of hundreds of thousands of men and women who struggled relentlessly each day just to stay alive.

This was not just a case of what Nematullah called "peasant fever." Only last winter Hasan had witnessed the people's hardships first hand. Traveling in the rural areas to purchase cloth, he had seen shoeless children, their grayish-white feet numb with cold; old men, their once-fierce pride now eroded as they spent long evenings scavenging for scraps of food; and shamefaced widows who had stooped to selling their daughters' virtue for a bag of rice. In some communities, for every child who lived beyond the age of five, another died; and for those who did manage to survive, life's blessing was little more than wanton misery: long hours in the dusty fields, sleepless nights in inadequate shelter, and monotonous meals on rationlike provisions—flat bread and yogurt, nothing more. Even in the more prosperous families, food was scarce. Extras were virtually unknown, and meat had become a holy-day luxury. As for quantity, the breakfast Nematullah had consumed earlier that morning would have fed a family for several days.

"This is a crime," whispered Hasan. What was worse, he knew that, compared to the treatment given the shah, this display was nothing.

By this time, Nematullah had made his way to the royal presence to proclaim that all was ready. Standing in front of the prince, his hands filled with golden coin, he awaited the announcement of the Master of Ceremonies, whose voice soon droned throughout the compound. "The meanest of your servants, O Prince, O Son of the Shadow of God on Earth, desires to make a presentation. The owner of this caravanserai, Nematullah-i Bastami, begs that he might approach Your Highness and make a humble offering of fifty *tumáns.*

Nonchalantly nodding his assent without dismounting, the prince watched as Nematullah handed the gold coins to an attendant and knelt to kiss the dirt in front of him. "You are undoubtedly a faithful servant," the nobleman mumbled without changing his facial expression. "Your gift is, by our grace, accepted."

"Thank you, O Illustrious One; may my life be sacrificed for you," replied Nematullah, rising. "Please enter this humble abode and bestow upon my family eternal honor."

Surrounded by his entourage, the prince began the short journey into the garden, the piles of carpets and cloth passing rapidly behind his black riding boots. Behind him a small army of attendants scrambled to gather up the valuable merchandise. Taking most of the homespun garments for themselves, they carefully avoided any plunder of the silks or brocades.

In the midst of this thievery, Hasan's eye was caught by a child's rough little coat which had been thrown to

26

the ground in the confusion. Quilted to protect its small owner from the winter frost, the garment's edges had been decorated with tiny brocade flowers—evidence of a mother's loving handiwork. Now the effort of half the summer lay in the busy thoroughfare, unnoticed in the mad contest to grab the more costly prizes. Only the onlooking peasant children seemed aware of its existence. But none of them found the courage to dash out and grab it.

Seeing these small, half-naked frames, Hasan felt that his legs were ready to give away. Grabbing hold of the low wall in front of him, he steadied himself and tried to clear his thoughts. "I must go down," he eventually sputtered, and as the prince neared his destination the young man found his way to the exterior stairs and descended to the garden below.

By the time he had reached the ground, the prince was already seated. Merging quietly into the crowd of onlookers, Hasan did his best to look unobtrusive. He knew that Nematullah would be searching for him, hoping that the prince might condescend to receive his younger brother. He shuddered at the thought. I don't think he will see me here, he thought. At least I hope not.

Moments later, the Master of Ceremonies' voice once again began to ring through the courtyard, quieting the crowd and drawing attention to his next announcement. "As a tribute to His Highness Prince Bahram, Mírzá Yusuf has been given the honor of sharing some of his verse."

With this introduction, the Court Poet humbly approached the foot of the dais. From the tip of his high-pointed shoes to the top of his gold-laced silk vest he was every inch a courtier. Skilled almost since birth in the art of flattery, he was well prepared for the occasion.

"Whatever the prince desires," he began, "is evidence of his wisdom." Turning to song, he began to reveal his prepared verse.

> Like the stars that sprinkle the sky,
> the king's sons illumine the land of Persia.
>
> Wherever they go, they bring light
> like the sun.
>
> The owner of this caravanserai
> can boast of fine accommodation.
>
> But what accommodation is equal
> to the prince's presence?
>
> What are all the luxuries of life
> compared to the presence of the prince?
>
> O Nematullah-i Bastami, most honored of men,
> worry not about future success.
>
> The Prince of Princes has your life blessed.

When the poet had finished, the assembly waited in anticipatory silence, fearful that any display on their part might usurp the royal prerogative. Then, in a low-toned but firm voice, the prince gave his verdict. "You have done very well," he said with a look of self-indulgent satisfaction. "You are indeed a poet worthy of our favor."

As the poet took a deep bow, the prince turned to one of his attendants and ordered him to fill the courtier's mouth with fine sugared candies, a task which the servant performed with great pomp and ceremony. The result was a broad smile and another ingratiating bow from the poet.

As soon as the courtier had slunk back among the myriad of attendants, the prince signaled to the Master of Ceremonies that he desired silence. The man responded instantly with a third blast of his vocal cords. "O servants of the King of Kings! Prince Bahram will now speak. All remain quiet!"

The prince gently cleared his throat. Assuming an officious posture he addressed the crowd. "O sons of Persia! As all of you well know, this country is one which, from the beginning of the world, has been blessed by the excellence of its monarchs. My father, Muḥammad S̲h̲áh, may the blessings of the Prophet remain upon him, is a fine example of the genius of such rule. His wisdom and intelligence have made Persia the envy of the entire world. His well-organized and efficient administration is admired from India to Turkey—and even the western infidels come to him bearing presents and tribute. In his most august wisdom, he has recently seen fit to appoint me governor of this province. As his loyal son, I will see to it that the glory which resides in Tehran, the magnificent hub of the empire, will also become manifest here."

Pausing for a moment to gather his thoughts, the speaker stared skyward. Then, once again lowering his eyes, he continued. "In governing a province, help is needed from many quarters. As a gift from the Center of the Universe—the King of Kings—loyal citizens of the realm are on occasion given the privilege of assisting in the administration of affairs. It has come to our attention that the owner of this caravanserai is such a man, and we therefore present him here today with a royal *farmán* granting him the title of District Tax Assessor. From this day forward, he shall help us in establishing the amount of revenue to be sent from this province to the Royal Treasury in Tehran."

As the last words of his speech gently echoed off the surrounding walls, the prince turned to another of his aides, who promptly handed him a sealed scroll. Taking it in his hand, he motioned to yet another attendant, who in turn directed the waiting Nematullah to approach the dais. Humbly walking forward, his hands folded together in front of his massive chest, his head slightly bowed, the new appointee reached the base of the portable throne. Still keeping his eyes lowered, he reached forward to receive the scroll.

"May you perform your task well," proclaimed the prince as he placed the *farmán* into the outstretched hand.

"And may God always shower you and your family with His grace," responded Nematullah respectfully.

His boon in hand, Nematullah dutifully lowered himself to the ground and, for a second time that day, placed his closed lips lightly against the soft earth. Watching him, Hasan was filled with disgust. How could he humiliate himself so?

Prince Bahram did not bother to look at the prone figure of his new assessor. He simply dismissed him with a quick wave of his hand and leaned forward to consult with the Master of Ceremonies. As their discussion continued, Hasan became aware of footsteps behind him. Turning around, he saw a line of servants moving toward the royal tent. As he suspected, they were delivering the fare which the royal cooks had spent the entire afternoon preparing. As they passed by, their overflowing silver platters revealed an ensemble of culinary delights. The rices alone took up a dozen trays: four or five different pilafs, some containing pieces of boiled lamb, others heavy with baked fowl, and still others sprinkled with shreds of orange peel, slivered almonds, and spices. These were followed by a variety of fish dishes including salmon, herring, and trout all prepared in the most exotic sauces. Then came a number of large omelettes, some made with herbs and onions, and others with prunes and lamb. Next appeared plates of poached eggs topped with melted butter and sugar; and behind them more stews of chicken and venison.

For a moment there was a break in the procession, and Hasan thought that the gluttonous display was over. But soon a second wave of platters appeared. The first trays carried the roasts: a full spitted lamb, numerous pheasants and several Persian partridges. Following these were choice cuts of antelope and ox, the steaks artistically surrounded by hundreds of pickles, onions and peppers, fashioned in the shapes of different wild animals. After several dozen bowls of mixed fruits, and a similar amount of curd, there at last appeared the sherbets: seven varieties in all, from lemon to pomegranate, each perfumed with rosewater and cooled by large chunks of ice.

"The court will consume in one evening more than a month's provisions for three villages," Hasan said under his breath. "And Nematullah has stolen most of it."

By now the conversation between the prince and the Master of Ceremonies had ceased, and the latter was preparing himself to make yet another announcement. "As a blessing from the Royal Family," he cried, loudly clapping his hands together, "as a blessing from the Royal Family, the Luminous Moon of the King of Kings, Prince Bahram, has consented to hear any petitions which might be offered up from his loyal subjects. If there be someone in attendance who would wish address the royal personage, let him do so now."

Several seconds of silence followed and it appeared that the imperial offer would go unanswered, when there abruptly appeared from the back of the throng a man dressed in riding trousers, a rough woolen shirt and a soiled, brown turban. At first, the Master of Ceremonies did not see him and was about to proclaim the formal part of the occasion over. But as he began to open his mouth, he spotted the lowly subject, and with a wave of his hand he summoned the man forward.

Hesitantly the petitioner approached the dais. Finally stopping, he looked up toward the surprised prince and humbly began to reveal his plight. "I am a groom in the stables of my master, Nematullah-i Bastami. This morning as I was preparing for Your Excellency's arrival, one of the royal attendants seized me and ordered upon threat of a beating that I give him the silver coin which my master had given me in honor of Your Lordship's visit. I now beg of Your Highness to order the man to return my coin."

When the groom had finished his story, the prince placed his hands on the side of the felt-covered throne. For the first time since his arrival at the platform, he raised himself to his feet. "Do you see this man here?" he inquired of the nervous subject.

"Yes, Your Excellency," responded the man.

"Where?"

"It is that man over there." He pointed to one of the petty officers of the stable standing to the left of the dais.

A quick nod of the prince's head in the direction of the Chief Tent Pitcher was all that was required. Moments later, a humiliated attendant stood cowering in front of his enraged master.

"You son of the devil," bawled the prince, "where is the money you stole from this man?"

"I swear I took nothing," answered the attendant meekly. "I have never seen him before."

"We shall see about that. Perhaps a beating of your feet will improve your memory." Waving his arm wildly in the air, the prince summoned his personal bodyguards.

The sight of the approaching black-coated officers, rods in hand, unnerved the attendant, and before they had time to carry out their task, he reached down into his boot and pulled forth the silver coin. Straightening up, he handed it to the Chief Tent Pitcher, who in turn passed it on to the prince.

Prince Bahram hardly glanced at the silver. With heavy breath he shouted out his orders. "Take this attendant away and give him the beating he deserves. Then take his uniform away from him; I never want to see him cross my sight again."

Instantaneously, the body guards seized the frightened servant by his shoulders and dragged him from the platform. Meanwhile, the prince had closed his jewel-laden hand around the coin and again seated himself on the throne. Looking down at the still-shaking groom, he growled, "You may leave."

"But what about my coin?"

"Watch your tongue," screamed the Master of Ceremonies as he struck the man in the face. "You should be grateful that Prince Bahram has accepted your gift. Now begone with you!"

Bewildered, the man hesitated and then turned to leave. "Do not turn your back on His Highness," bellowed the Master of Ceremonies. Removing his own shoe, he took several steps forward and again unloaded his wrath on the hapless groom. "Back away, as is respectful!" he yelled.

Reacting from fear rather than respect, the groom bowed awkwardly to the prince. Following the Master of Ceremonies' instructions, he backpeddled his way into the crowd.

By now, Hasan's disgust had turned to anger. Looking at his gloating brother, his hands automatically tightened. The nails of his fingers dug into his sweat-lined palms. Within, he could feel nothing but revulsion. So this is the nation he so adamantly supports, he thought contemptuously—a nation which fed its fat-faced court on the supplies of its starving peasantry; a nation whose royal family found its humor in the suffering of the lowly; a nation that allowed its officials to strip the local population like a swarm of locusts.

The young man's eyes were almost glazed. Couldn't Nematullah see through all this vulgarity? Did he really consider this spectacle a tribute to family honor? No, the only honor Nematullah knew was greed, and no sacrifice was too great to cast on this epicurean altar.

Hasan had seen enough. He could no longer stay in the presence of the prince and his own brother. It would be an insult to my sense of justice, he thought, clutching at his cramped stomach. And thus, as the son of the Center of the Universe led the way into the royal tent, Hasan took himself to the rear of the garden and silently slipped away.

Chapter 4

EVEN BEFORE THE SUN'S first rays began to filter into the room, Hasan lay awake on his bed. He had spent another restless night. In fact, he had not slept well since the departure of the prince. But the questions that returned to his mind time and again, and the ones he now pondered as he lay there in the silence of the early morning, were not related to the anger Nematullah had expressed at his rude departure from the banquet. Neither were they concerned with Amin. Amin was gone, and rant and rave as he might, Nematullah could do nothing about it. The question was, what should Hasan do? Should he follow his emotions and join his younger brother? But what if Nematullah was right? What if this sayyid was an imposter? How could one ever know for sure if a man who claimed a revelation from God was speaking the truth?

Still deep in thought, Hasan raised himself up from the bed, put on his robe, and headed downstairs. He liked to walk while he was thinking, and the present moment offered an excellent opportunity to leave the house unnoticed. Once below, he slipped out the door and hastily made his way toward the outer grounds of the compound. Passing through the empty rose garden, he entered the stables where he was greeted by several grooms preparing a number of horses for their morning departure. Noticeably absent was the stable hand who had had the nerve to report his misfortune to the prince. Where he had disappeared to, no one knew. Only his torn shirt, which had been found outside the caravanserai, remained as evidence that he once worked inside its walls.

Leaving the neighing of horses and the grooms' whistles and shouts behind him, Hasan wandered down the cobble-stone roadway in the direction of the old mosque. Some-how it all seemed strange, he thought: a man claiming to be the spokesman for God. In one sense, Nematullah was certainly right. It was easy to accept the Prophet Muḥammad as God's appointed messenger—history and tradition were behind such belief. In fact, one did not have to come to terms with the question at all. It was already answered for you by the mullás, the mujtahids, and your elders. But this was different. A man made of flesh and blood—not some shadowy ghost from the past—was making a claim, and the decision he called for lay squarely on the shoulders of each individual.

Hasan's thought had become so intense that he hardly noticed the scenery around him. When his eyes once again focused on the surroundings, he found himself only fifty paces away from the mosque. The sun, which by now was above the horizon, cast powerful streams of light on the structure's blue-tiled dome. And although most of the ceramic pieces were covered with a thin layer of dirt, they still managed to issue forth a mute sparkle.

The sight of the building reminded Hasan that in his anxiety he had forgotten to say his morning prayers. Per-haps this was part of the problem, he thought, the reason why he was having such a difficult time deciding on a course of action. By his nature he was not as spiritual as Amin. Pursuing this theme, he thought back to when they were only small children. He had always been the one who forgot to say his prayers, while Amin continued to delight their father by putting to memory over twenty suras of the Holy Qur'an. Now, fifteen years later, the legacy re-mained. For Amin, the spirit of the divine flowed freely from the heart, while for Hasan, God was primarily an object of thought.

He had now reached the mosque's outer wall. Walking through a narrow, cobwebbed archway, he came into the courtyard where visitors performed their ablutions. Spotting the lustration bowl, he veered toward it. After a few steps in the direction of the marble basin, his ears filled with the sound of a man's voice chanting holy verses. Quickly, he washed his hands, arms, and feet. Then, drawn by the voice, he approached the door leading into the building. At the threshold, he stopped to remove his shoes. Then, straightening his robe, he entered the inner sanctuary.

Once inside, his eyes focused on the source of the song. Some twenty feet away, kneeling on a small blue and white carpet, wearing only a scanty woolen garment tightly knotted around his loins, was a dervish feverishly reciting a Quranic chapter which Hasan instantly recognized as the Sura of Joseph. Mesmerized, he watched the unkempt, wild figure straining before him in religious passion. Periodically the dervish would leave his upright position and stretch out on his stomach in the direction of the *qiblih,* his long, tangled hair falling to the floor around him. Then, several seconds later, he would raise his body and assume a vertical posture, maintaining all the while his loud and sing-song tune.

After several minutes the chanting ended, and for another period of approximately equal length the man lay prostrate on the floor of the mosque, obviously exhausted by his efforts. Despite the fact that there was now silence in the building, Hasan still could not move: he could only stare in amazement at the scene before him. Finally, a slow movement of the hands, followed by a tightening of the

37

muscles in the back, signaled the man's ascent. In the next moment he was on his feet and heading toward Hasan and the doorway. Almost immediately the dervish spotted the intruder, but without hesitating he riveted his eyes upon him and continued forward. The sight of the bizarre figure bearing down on him caused Hasan some alarm. His natural impulse was to bolt, but the man's eyes so dominated him that he stood stationary as a rooted tree in the doorway.

When he was only a few feet away, the dervish stopped and looked into Hasan's face. "God is Most Great!" he blurted out. "Don't let me stop you from your prayers."

The sudden burst of sound surprised Hasan, and without taking time to think he said, "I did not intend to pray."

The dervish continued to focus his powerful eyes on those of Hasan, but now a look of compassion crept over his dirt-lined face. "You are troubled, my brother."

As if speaking to an old friend, Hasan answered the dervish's unspoken question without reflection. "I have a decision to make, and I am finding it hard to come to a satisfactory conclusion."

"Come." The holy man did not wait for a response, but turned and started out the door.

Like a puppy following its master, Hasan instinctively heeded his suggestion by accompanying him into the sunlight. Once outside, the two men passed through the courtyard, under the archway, and beyond the wall to the row of cedar trees that lined the roadway. There, amid the fallen yellow leaves of the pomegranate bushes, they sat down.

"What is it that is causing you such severe anxiety, my friend?" asked the dervish.

Although he had just met the man, the dervish's sincere

and straightforward manner impressed Hasan. Thus, despite the fact that his question was personal, the young man had no hesitation in answering. "It concerns my younger brother. He has gone east to join the disciples of Sayyid 'Alí-Muḥammad. Have you heard of him?"

"I believe that he is called the Báb by his followers, is he not?" replied the dervish.

Hasan nodded.

"Well, your brother is obviously a man searching for his God. Why should that cause you anxiety?"

"I only wish that my older brother agreed with you," sighed Hasan.

"What has he to do with it?"

"He is the head of the family. When our father died, my brother, along with my uncle who lives in Tehran, took charge of our welfare. He feels that this sayyid is a fool, if not an imposter."

"I see," the dervish said. "And how did your younger brother get involved with the heretics?"

"A few years ago, when we were living in Shiraz, one night he had a dream. He saw himself approaching a man whom he had never seen before. The stranger was a young sayyid with delicate, almost womanlike features. He was dressed in the finest cloth of pure white. The man stood under a dead tree—or perhaps it was winter, since the tree had no leaves. In any case, Amin noticed that in the bare, black branches of the tree a severed head hung above the young man's form. He instantly recognized it as the head of the martyred Imám Ḥusayn and was overcome by a feeling of awe and reverence."

"From the nature of your account," said the dervish, "it might have been your own dream, rather than your brother's."

"Amin later described the dream to me in great detail,"

Hasan explained, "and I will never forget it. But, it does not end here. The young sayyid gazed on the face of the beloved Ḥusayn and began to chant the Sura of Joseph from the Qur'an, the very sura you were chanting in the mosque a few minutes ago. As he chanted, Amin realized that his words carried great meaning, but he could understand none of it. Oh, the words were from the Qur'an, of course, but they seemed to have a higher meaning that Amin could not penetrate."

"It is indeed highly allegorical." The dervish picked his nose thoughtfully.

"Then Amin saw a few drops of blood fall from the severed head. The sayyid gathered the blood on the finger-tips of his right hand and brought it to his lips, as a sign of devotion. When he did so, his face was transformed into light."

The dervish was about to comment when the sound of approaching horses caused both men to look up. Coming up the roadway toward them was a group of four riders.

"No doubt a party of merchants returning to the capital," suggested Hasan aloud.

As the riders cantered by, they offered their morning salutations. The two men responded with similar gestures. Seconds later the party passed. The interruption over, the dervish resumed the dialog.

"A very strange dream," he murmured.

"Even stranger things were to happen," said Hasan. "The next day an unknown man came into our shop, handed Amin a note, and vanished just as quickly as he had entered. The note, which was immaculately written, as if by a calligrapher, was an invitation to share an evening meal with a man whose name Amin did not recognize. For a while he wavered as to whether he should go, but the combination of interest and intrigue finally convinced him. He set out later, note in hand, to find its author. Following the directions, he found himself at the gate of a modest house. As he neared the door he was met by an Ethiopian servant who ushered him inside. He was then led to a small room where he encountered his host. Seated on the floor, wearing the green turban of a sayyid, he was chanting the Sura of Joseph. Without a doubt, Amin knew who he was."

"The sayyid in the dream—Sayyid 'Alí-Muḥammad?"

"Yes."

"And what happened next?"

"They spoke for some time. The sayyid gave him a copy of his commentary on the sura, telling Amin that God would surely guide seekers of truth. Then, he departed."

"Did Amin ever meet him again?"

"No. About a week later the sayyid was forced to leave the city. The local mullás had threatened him with violence."

"Where did he go?"

"Amin learned that he had gone to Isfahan. Not long after, the sayyid was arrested by order of the Crown. Since that time, his followers have been openly persecuted. Many of them have been forced to flee to the east."

"This is certainly very interesting," the dervish said after a few moments of reflective silence. "But in all honesty, I don't see what you are worrying about. Amin is gone, and nothing you or your older brother can do will change that. All things are due to the will of God."

"That may well be," retorted Hasan, "but there is more to it than I have thus far told you. You see, I myself am thinking of joining Amin."

"Then you believe in this Qá'im?"

Hasan peered down the roadway, trying to organize his thoughts. "To be honest," he finally answered, "I am not sure what it means to believe. All I know is that this man has greatly affected Amin, and his commentary shows that he has great spiritual power: this cannot be denied. I have found that I hate the corruption and hypocrisy of this society. I need something that can give my life meaning. Perhaps I am hoping I can find it among these men. In any case, if I spend the rest of my life in a cloth shop, I will never know."

"And it is your older brother's attitude toward this sayyid that is keeping you from leaving?"

"He will not even accept the fact that Amin has gone. God knows what he would do if I told him that I was leaving as well."

"But what can he do?" repeated the dervish. "He can't stop you from leaving."

"I know that." Hasan frowned. "But I guess you could say I feel a responsibility to him. He has just been appointed District Assessor by virtue of a royal *farmán*, and family honor is paramount in his mind. He would like me to get married and have children . . . to do those things which provide the foundations for wealth and family."

"Then what will you say to God on the Day of Judgment?" exclaimed the dervish, suddenly becoming extremely serious. "Will you tell Him: 'I put my brother and his wishes before You'?"

The holy man's words cut Hasan like a knife. He felt a twinge of anger, and for an instant he thought of leaving. But he knew that the dervish was right. If a man was not honest with himself, and lived only in response to the wishes of others, he had thrown away his soul. He felt a refreshing wave rush through his body: he had made his decision. "What you say is true," he whispered. "I must go. I will inform Nematullah this very evening."

"God is Most Great," said the dervish. "I can travel with you as far as the capital."

"Then why don't you join me, and find out more about this Qá'im for yourself?" responded Hasan, hoping that he had found a traveling companion for the arduous journey east.

"No, my dear friend," answered the dervish, shaking his head. "I have already found my God, and no Qá'im will change that. But you have not found yours. These things must be done alone. But, God willing, I will meet you here tomorrow morning at dawn."

"But where will you sleep?"

"Don't worry about me. God's love is my dwelling."

"I will bring you a horse."

"As you like, my friend." Wishing Hasan God's blessing, the dervish rose to his feet and started back toward the mosque.

Chapter 5

ALI UNDID THE LATCH on the shop's door. Slowly swinging it open, he stepped quietly into the dark room. His head still experienced a mellow sensation from the wine he had been consuming most of the evening. As he passed the stacked rows of cloth lining the shop's interior, he felt as if he were floating. Continuing to the back of the room, the well-built, fully bearded young man reached a curtained partition which separated the remainder of the shop from his sleeping area. Drawing back the cloth wall, he took two more steps before allowing himself to drop limply on his bed.

As he lay silently in the darkness, he wondered if he would get the opportunity to catch a glimpse of his employer's wife. Earlier in the day he had heard the owner of the shop announce that he would leave Qum for several days on another of his business trips. He was sure that she would be alone. Whether she would bring herself out of the inner part of the house, however, he did not know.

Rolling over on his elbow, Ali lit the small brass lamp on the rough wood table beside his bed. Once the light started to flicker, he leaned back to reflect on this woman whom he had never really seen. For weeks he had watched her scurrying in and out of the house on her way to the bazaar, her loosely hung mesh veil revealing tantalizing flashes of her partially covered face. Once, he was certain that she had seen him staring and had responded with a slight nod. Now, in the inner sanctum of his mind her alluring, phantomlike figure was enticing him, seducing his soul.

In the midst of this fantasy, a beam of light burst through the partly opened doorway that led from his own room into the kitchen. Could it be? he wondered.

Normally his hope would have ended here, but the euphoria that the alcohol had induced gave him a feeling of bravado that he did not usually possess. Quickly rising from his bed, he cautiously approached the door and peeked in.

No sooner had his eyes adjusted to the inner light than he saw her. Stooping over as she prepared tea, her black veil was cast back behind her head. She revealed a face whose features were haunting and attractive. She was not beautiful—her eyes were too close together and her nose too long to fit the canons of classical beauty. But her dark brown skin, full lips, and rich black hair gave her a compelling sensuality which instantly captivated her admirer. Reacting as if mesmerized, Ali inadvertently grabbed the door.

The unexpected movement startled the young woman, and she reacted by jumping in fright and pulling the veil over her face. "Why are you staring at me? You must go away!"

But the tone of her voice indicated to Ali that the command was dictated more by custom than desire. Boldly leaning forward he pushed his way into the doorway.

"My husband is gone," the woman said coldly. "You should not be here."

"Perhaps we can share the tea," responded Ali as if he had not heard her. "Your name is Shahin, isn't it?"

"Yes." Hesitantly accepting Ali's invitation, she went to the samovar and poured tea into two small glasses.

"My name is Ali," said the young man, watching her.

"I know. I have heard my husband mention your name."

Ali could feel by the rising heat in his face that he was beginning to blush. Searching for something else on which his excited mind could focus, he thought of the tea. But as he was about to reach for the glass, the woman once again began to speak.

"I also know that you are not from Qum."

"My father sent me here from Shiraz," said Ali, forgetting the tea. "He sent me to stay with my uncle, Mullá Mahmudi. Perhaps you know him?"

"My husband often speaks of him. He is a very religious man."

Although Ali was not used to talking to a woman, he now felt surprisingly at ease. Despite the fact that Shahin had become quiet behind her veil, he felt compelled to explain his situation in greater detail. "My father sent me here to Qum because in Shiraz I was neglectful of my religious duties. He wanted me to become a mullá. No doubt he thought that my uncle could be of some help. But as far as I am concerned, religion is the curse of our country, and the mullás are the curse of religion. In taking this position I was greatly influenced by a book which I had received from a good friend of mine who had known the author, a western physician residing in Shiraz. He had taken it upon himself to translate it into our tongue. The book dealt with a large number of subjects, but essentially it set out the views of western scholars and physicians on such topics as religion and science, comparing them to the more established ideas of tradition. The point of the arguments presented was that religion was superstition, a remnant of primitive thinking about the world, and a barrier to progress."

"But you were supposed to become a mullá," gasped Shahin, her interest aroused.

"Yes," replied Ali. "But several weeks with my uncle confirmed my unbelief even more. His world was the narrow world of the mosque. He spent his days praying and his nights studying the law: of life he knew nothing."

"I see."

"At first he insisted I go with him daily to the mosque. But when he saw that this regulation was having the opposite of its intended effect, and only making me more rebellious, he softened his stance and only made me go on Fridays. I had to promise, however, that I would follow my religious duties and perform the obligatory daily prayers. To tell the truth, I think that he finally resigned himself to the fact that I was lost—one of the damned—for soon afterwards he arranged for my employment in your husband's shop."

"But you spend a great deal of time away from the shop," Shahin said. "Aren't you afraid that my husband will say something to the mullá?"

"I believe your husband is too kind to say anything. He probably feels that my uncle would take the actions of his nephew as a personal failure. And this burden he would not place on his friend."

"Yes, he is a kind man . . . but where do you go when you leave the shop?"

"I have friends in the bazaar. Sometimes we drink wine or smoke hashish, but we talk about interesting things . . . about life. When I am there I feel free and exhilarated—not like here, where the most exciting thing that can happen to you is the establishment of a new account."

"Then why don't you leave?" asked Shahin bluntly.

"Interesting that you ask. Just tonight my friend Javad was telling us about a young sayyid from Shiraz who is challenging the authority of the mullás. He wants me to go with him to seek out this man, but I know my uncle would never permit it. I long to go, to see life as it really is. Yet I am cooped up like a bird in a cage.''

Ali lowered his head and contemplated the incompatibility of his dreams and the situation in which he found himself. At the same time, he was conscious of Shahin's unbroken, though veil-hidden, gaze. In an effort to remove himself from the center of attention, he finally looked up and spoke. "But I have said enough about my life. What about yourself?''

With these words Shahin seemed to change. The sparkle went out of her voice and her head drooped. She no longer looked at Ali, but cast her glance down at the floor. In a tone that impressed the young man as unspeakably sad she said, "You speak of yourself as a bird in a cage. That is how I feel. You see, I am from Bushir. I was married to my husband against my wishes. As you know, he is much older than I. He lost his first wife two years back, and my father, who is a good friend of his, offered me to him. I protested, but it was to no use. Now I am here in a strange city, in the back of a cloth shop, away from all family and friends. My only companions are the four walls.''

As Ali looked at the young woman, a feeling of deep compassion flooded his soul. He felt like reaching out and caressing her, but he could not. It was not that women were new to him—he had known several in the bazaars— but this was a married woman, the wife of his employer. In spite of his earlier fantasies, when confronted with reality his courage failed him. All he could do was sit impotent and still.

"It is not that he is a cruel man," continued Shahin abruptly. "As you said earlier, he is very kind. It is just that he does not really love me . . . and that is understandable. It is my duty to serve him . . . and he needs a companion, not a lover. His true love is this shop and his business.''

No longer could she hold back her emotions. All the feelings she had been trying to hide broke loose. From behind her veil, large torrents of tears began to spill from her eyes, and her throat became filled with one continual sob. Watching from the other side of the table, Ali felt helpless. She was like an injured bird who needed to be protected, but it was not his place to do so. What should I do? he kept asking himself, mentally cursing the customs that caused such suffering. She needs warmth, affection . . . And then it no longer seemed to matter.

"God forgive me," he murmured. Reaching out, he took Shahin by the shoulders and gently pulled her toward him.

In Ali's arms, Shahin began to quiet herself. Gradually her sobbing quieted, and soon only a periodic whimper issued forth from her once-trembling frame. Listening to the throbbing of her heart against his chest, the young man's pulse began to quicken. He fought the temptation to raise her head to his. No! he thought. No! *Not now!* But his own effort at self-restraint was undone by the woman herself who, anticipating his feeling, tilted her neck invitingly backward.

Ali's reply was instantaneous. Gently lifting her head, he removed the free-hanging veil and placed his full, beard-lined lips over hers. Like an impatient bride, she responded with uncontrolled passion.

"Come with me," Ali said, raising his head and looking longingly into her dark brown eyes. Unable to hold herself back, Shahin took the young man's hand, and forgetting her wifely duty, followed him into his darkened room.

ALI LAY PROSTRATE on the floor of his uncle's mosque, repeating over and over the phrase "God is Most Great." He had been doing this for over an hour now, and he had promised himself that he would keep repeating the verse until he received an answer. He was alone in the spacious sanctuary. Although the sun had long since set, he was determined to remain in the domain of the Almighty the entire night if necessary.

As the words flowed from his mouth, the young man tried as hard as he could to concentrate on his own mental image of God and to banish the furies of reflection from his mind. Yet, despite his effort, they kept returning in periodic flashes, inserting themselves in between the words of his prayer: Shahin, her sad, alluring eyes; her husband, busily working behind the counter of his shop, unaware of his helper's perfidious act; his uncle, announcing to the family Shahin's death . . . Once again the pain of this last image cut into his soul like a knife. Why? he silently cried. Then, remembering his promise, he fought with all his might to think only of God, the Forgiver, the All-Compassionate.

It had been three months now since that fatal evening when his uncle had revealed the news of his lover's death. Only two days before, he had left the merchant's shop for good, unable to endure any longer the conflict eating at the center of his being. He loved her, but it was impossible. Rather than daily confront the agony of separation, he had decided to depart and take his pain with him. They had been two days of melancholy and gloom. But when he heard his uncle's words, the melancholy turned to anguish, and with each passing day the pit of inner despair into which he had fallen grew deeper.

Not only was he greatly bereaved over the death of the woman he loved, now the gnawing pangs of guilt about his own involvement in the tragedy began to haunt him. Again and again he tried to assure himself that it was not his fault: improper though his actions were, he could not be held responsible for what had followed. He had not made her any promises. If anything, it was fate. Yet, rationalize as he might, he knew something was wrong. It was too easy to argue away one's own responsibility. Perhaps she had become pregnant and could not face the shame of confronting her husband? Or maybe he had driven her to despair of her own life? But she was already sad, and he hadn't caused that. He was caught in the vicious circle of speculation and thought.

In desperation, Ali had turned to God. What had once seemed to him an intellectual absurdity soon became an emotional necessity. He passed the following days at the mosque, praying, meditating, searching. He wanted assurance that he was forgiven. However, rather than alleviate his guilt, the effort plunged him further into despondency. One day, after he had spent most of the morning reading from the Qur'an, a terrible fear came over him: perhaps his uncle had been right—perhaps he was damned?

Through the next few weeks he became obsessed with this possibility. Instinctively, he called on his intellect to prove to himself that hell was inconceivable, a theological abomination. To his horror, he found that his intellect was impotent. There was nothing illogical about hell, no inherent contradiction. Perhaps it was absurd to think that such a place existed, yet this was no proof of its nonexistence. Maybe, he kept thinking, the universe is absurd. Why must it follow the laws of logic? And soon he lost all faith in reason. He was groundless, without foundation, locked in the depths of spiritual torment. Worst of all, there was no escape from the source of that torment: himself.

Days passed without him taking more than a morsel of

food; sleep came only with exhaustion. Hallucinations of the Day of Judgment filled his mind: standing shamefully in front of God, the entire creation gazing upon his exposed being. There was nowhere to run or to hide. The Almightly was irreconcilably angry with him, and him alone. All he could do was cringe and silently endure the humiliation of ultimate scorn.

It was with this cancerous growth festering in his soul that Ali had come to the mosque that morning, having decided that he would either resolve the conflict or end his own life. He knew that if there was an answer, he had to find it within the next twenty-four hours; if not, he would pay for his crimes. He would not grovel any longer in the quagmire of unredeemed self.

Unaware of the turmoil that his young nephew was experiencing, Ali's uncle did not take the lad's changed behavior seriously. Rather, he shrugged it off as another of his passing fantasies which would doubtlessly end as soon as he found another object of interest. Thus, although he was pleased when he found Ali spending much of his time at the mosque, he made no effort to guide him. Consequently, when Qum's evening shadows began to fall and Ali informed the mullá of his desire to remain alone, the elder divine did not protest. He merely departed with these words of advice: "Make sure that you do not play games with God. For He is surely the God of Wrath and Might." That had been four hours ago. Now Ali was once again immersed in the fires of spiritual struggle, trying as best he could to banish from his mind all but the name of God.

Another two hours passed, as Ali plunged deeper and deeper into despair. The abyss into which he had fallen had no end: the more he cried out for mercy, the greater became the searing flames of conscience. Although the evening was cooled by a gentle southerly breeze, the young man could not feel its comfort. Sweat covered his face, and his breathing became heavy. Unconsciously, his entire body began to writhe and wriggle, making him appear like a dying insect. Again he cried out: "Blessed be He in Whose hands is the creation, He Who created death and life to prove which of you is best in actions. He is the Mighty, the Ever Forgiving." Still the pain did not go away. Then his head began to spin, and a feeling of nausea gripped his insides. He wanted to vomit, but now not even his muscles would cooperate. He could only lie there, convulsing in his own sickness.

Trying desperately to regain his equilibrium, Ali summoned up all his mental strength and stared at a small crack in the floor just beneath him. For more than twenty minutes he remained in this position, holding on to what seemed the last remnants of sanity. Gradually the dizziness began to diminish, and his vision cleared. He now realized that his efforts had been to no avail. God's silence had told him what he wanted to know: he was condemned. There was only one path left. With this thought firm in his mind, he slowly raised himself to his knees and reached into his robe.

His hand touched the leather binding of his knife, and with one quick movement he pulled the sacrificial instrument into the open air.

The blade gave off a faint sparkle in the mosque's candle-lit sanctuary, and for a brief moment Ali's thoughts returned to Shahin's face. Catching himself, he hastily emptied his mind. He gathered up all his courage and raised the shiny steel to his sweat-soaked neck. With the blade resting on his pounding jugular vein, he closed his eyes and prepared for the last violent pull of the arm downward.

Just as he was about to convert his will into action, he heard a noise behind him. Quickly, he concealed the weapon in his robe and turned around to investigate the sound. The image which confronted him was that of Javad. His friend was standing in the doorway, breathing heavily and peering into the sanctuary. "Is that you, Ali?" he asked.

"Y-yes, it is me, Javad," stuttered Ali, still trying to regain his composure. "What do you want?"

"I am leaving to find out more about the young Shirazi sayyid, 'Alí-Muḥammad. Your uncle told me you were here, and I have come to ask you to join me."

Although Ali had clearly heard his friend, he did not answer. Expectantly looking down, Javad repeated his question. But Ali remained in a trancelike state.

"Ali?" called Javad apprehensively, as he left the doorway and began to approach his kneeling companion, "Ali?"

Still there was no answer. Only the sound of gentle breathing assured Javad that he was not alone.

"Ali?" he again whispered, but his friend did not stir. And for another three minutes Javad was forced to stand helplessly by as the figure before him looked blankly into inner space.

Slowly, as if waking from a dream, Ali began to shake his head. With tears freely flowing down his cheeks, he looked up. "Yes, I will join you," he said.

54

Chapter 6

THE SOUND OF a galloping horse alerted the two men sitting in the shaded garden. Jumping to their feet, they looked down the dirt road leading from the quiet grove to the small hamlet of Badasht. Within seconds they were able to make out the figure of a single horseman rapidly coming toward them.

"Were we expecting anyone?" asked the man robed in black.

"Not that I know of," responded his gray-clad partner. "I thought everyone had already arrived."

As they watched, the rider reached the outskirts of the small compound. Pulling back on the reins of his frothing steed, he brought the animal to a slow trot and continued forward slowly toward the suspicious eyes of the guards. When he was only a few feet away, he stopped and called out his greeting. "God's blessing be upon you. I have come to find Amin-i Bastami. Pray, tell me if he is here?"

"What do you want with him?" replied the man in black, his cautiousness causing him to put normal courtesy aside.

"He is my brother," answered Hasan. "I have come from Mashhad, where I was told that I would find him here."

Hasan sensed from the silence which greeted his response that his listeners were still apprehensive. "I have been staying with Mírzá Baqir. He sent me."

"Then you are certainly welcome," said the sentry, his broad smile breaking the tension. "I am Rashid and this is

55

Husayn. Come, join us in our refreshment. It is a long ride from Mashhad; you must be thirsty."

Gratefully responding to the invitation, Hasan dismounted and followed the two guards to the shade of a nearby garden, whose enclosure was filled with conversing men.

"Please," said Rashid handing the guest a cup of lemon water. "Amin is nearby. I will get him and see to it that your horse is watered and washed down."

Hasan thanked his host and hurriedly drank the cooling liquid. Observing the seated men from his position beneath a sprawling oak tree, he was struck by the appearance of one in particular. I know that face, he thought. I know that face. Then, slowly, behind the scruffy beard, a familiar image took shape. "Yes, that is him," he muttered under his breath. Unable to hold back his revelation, he announced it for all to hear. "Ali!"

The sound of his name ringing through the garden surprised Ali. He looked in the direction of the voice and for several long seconds studied its owner. Could it be? he wondered. Is it? And then he blurted out his thought. "Is it Hasan-i Bastami?"

"Yes, it is I," responded the excited Hasan. Moving toward Ali, he engulfed him with a warm and affectionate hug. "But whatever are you doing here?" he asked.

"I came here with a companion to seek out the followers of Sayyid-i Báb," replied Ali. "And you?"

"I have come to find my brother. You must have met him?"

"Yes, I have. But he has certainly changed since I knew him in Shiraz."

"Haven't we all."

"I still remember the day you left," said Ali, the quickness of his speech revealing his excited state. It was a very sad occasion for me."

"And for me as well," said Hasan. "But as you know, the death of our father completely altered our lives. Shiraz was too far removed from the rest of the family. My mother wanted to be closer to Nematullah, and since her brother was living in the capital . . . but there is no need to go into all of that. Tell me, what has happened to you since the last time we saw each other?"

"Like you, I eventually left Shiraz. My departure, however, was not of my own desire. Just about a year ago my father sent me to live with my uncle in Qum."

"The mullá?"

"Yes."

"Then how did you come to seek out the Báb?"

"It is largely due to my friend Javad," said Ali, turning and placing his hand on his companion's shoulder. "It was he who wanted to find out more about the sayyid."

Hasan realized that Ali's action was intended as a form of introduction. He instinctively held his hand over his heart and turned in the direction of the brown-robed, gray-turbaned man. At the same time, he looked into his narrow but strongly featured face and honored his presence with a short bowing of the head, a gesture to which Javad responded by doing likewise.

As Hasan and Javad completed their ritual, the sounds of approaching footsteps could be heard in the distance. Looking up, Hasan could tell immediately that it was his brother. Without a moment's hesitation, he enthusiastically cried out his name.

For an instant Amin broke his stride, squinting to see

if his ears had fooled him. Realizing that they had not, he launched himself forward into Hasan's waiting arms.

At first inspection, Amin's wide shoulders and broad forehead made him appear as if he was unrelated to the brother around whom his long arms were tenderly wrapped. But a close examination of his facial features revealed that he was indeed of the same stock. Only the softness of his cheeks and his clean-shaven chin and neck were distinctive. Otherwise, the deeply inset eyes, the high cheekbones, and the slightly curved nose were identical.

"I am surprised to see you here," exclaimed Amin as the two brothers pulled away from each other.

"Yes, I can understand that," said Hasan. "I finally decided that I should come here and find out more about this sayyid of yours for myself."

"If you have come to find out about our Master, Sayyid-i Báb," said Ali, "You have chosen the right time to arrive. There is much discussion going on at the moment as to the nature of his claims."

"He claims to be the Qá'im, does he not?" Hasan's voice rose to a new level of seriousness.

"Many are saying that he is only the gate to the hidden Imam," said Javad abruptly. "But there are some of us who believe that he is the Qá'im himself."

"How can he be the Qá'im?" interjected a white-robed, dark-skinned man sitting a few feet away. "Would the Qá'im have allowed himself to be captured and imprisoned?"

The aggressive tone with which the man made his comment raised Javad's ire. Without hesitating he angrily shot back, "Was not Muḥammad himself driven from Mecca?"

"But the Qá'im will be victorious over the entire world,"

the man retorted in a similarly vehement manner. "The powers of injustice will not be able to check him, even for an instant. Sayyid-i Báb—May the peace of God be upon Him—has only come to prepare the way for the Qá'im's advent. Such are the teachings of our Holy Book."

The nodding of heads and approving exclamations indicated that most of the men were in agreement with the man's sentiments. Only Amin, his youthful, beardless face flushed with agitation, thought of challenging the remarks. But just as he was about to join the conversation, an aging, black-turbaned man sitting directly behind Ali expounded his own thoughts. "I agree with what our companion is saying. When I was in Shiraz, I heard with my own ears Sayyid-i Báb deny any such claim."

"You ignorant fools," shouted Javad in frustration.

In an instant the dark-skinned man was on his feet, seemingly ready to resolve the argument with his fists. Only Amin's sudden intervention prevented a scuffle. Stepping between Javad and his attacker, he raised his voice to a virtual yell. "Friends!"

While the two antagonists calmed themselves, the rest of the companions turned their attention toward Amin, whose posture and countenance indicated that he was now ready to speak. Peering up at his brother, Hasan could not keep himself from thinking how much Amin had grown up. He is no longer a boy, the older brother reflected.

"With all due respect," began Amin, "I am afraid I cannot agree with the two previous statements. From what I have just heard, it is apparent that some of you have sacrificed the spirit of the message of God for the letter. Our friends here speak as if God's hand can be tied up. Yet did not the Apostle of God himself—peace be upon him—curse those who asserted that God's hand could be tied up? What I am hearing is the talk of orthodox theology, and we should not be so ignorant as to confuse the pretensions of theology with true religion.''

Amin's remarks set in motion a flurry of ideas. Throughout the garden men turned to one another, expressing their opinions in small conversations. The young man, however, was not yet finished. Speaking over the rising clamor, he continued: ''These same questions arose at the time of the appearance of the Messenger of God. Did not the acknowledged theologians of his time call him an unbeliever, a madman and a deceiver? Did they not incite the people to banish him from their midst? Does not that most holy of books, the Qur'an, itself provide a convincing testimony to the fact that the leaders of religion, caught in the subtleties of their own theology, have always been the worst enemies of the Prophet? Does the Holy Book not say: 'Hearts have ye, wherewith ye understand not; eyes have ye, wherewith ye see not; and ears have ye, wherewith ye hear not. Ye are like cattle; yea, worse than cattle have ye gone astray.' ''

''But what of the fact I just mentioned?'' pleaded the older man now standing. ''There were many present who heard Sayyid-i Báb's denial, and that is not a matter of mere theology.''

''I myself have spoken to men who were there,'' said Amin, ''and there was nothing in his discourse that contradicts what I am saying here. If anything, His speech proved to many that He is greater than a mere Báb.''

''Then who do you say He is?'' asked Ali.

''It is not what I say,'' retorted Amin. ''In his own Tablet He says: *'I am the Primal Point from which have been generated all created things. I am the Countenance of God whose splendor can never be obscured, the Light of God whose radiance can never fade. Whoso recognizeth me, assurance and all good are in store for him, and whoso faileth to recognize me, infernal fire and all evil await him.'"*

When Amin had finished, he remained standing, his entire being aflame with the spirit of the words he had just spoken. Throughout the grove, the atmosphere remained charged with a new vitality. The short speech had thrown forth a challenge, and everyone present was forced to react. To the dark-skinned man he remained an ignorant, if enthusiastaic, youth; while his words stuck a more responsive chord with the older gentleman.

It was on Ali, however, that Amin had the greatest effect. As Ali had been concentrating on the ideas Amin was expounding, he was mysteriously transported back to his uncle's mosque and the night he had nearly taken his own life. Vividly he remembered the strange sensation he had felt when Javad had mentioned the Báb's name, and the almost immediate alleviation of his spiritual agony which those few moments had produced. During the entire trip east, he had wondered about that night. Now he intuitively felt that he understood. It was an act of grace: God had forgiven him his sins and shown him the way. Now it was his responsibility to respond.

As for Hasan, he was pulled in two directions. He very much admired the new dynamism that had taken hold of his brother. Amin had always been a pious soul, but he had never been so powerfully vocal. Yet, in spite of this respect, Hasan realized that the disciples of the Báb were not in agreement about their beloved leader. As he sat in the late afternoon sun contemplating the discussion he had just heard, he was not sure if the man about whom Amin spoke was the real Báb or a mere product of his brother's own zealous faith.

Such was the situation for the next several minutes— each man searching his soul for the reason he was at Badasht and how he felt about the station of the incarcerated Master. So intense was the concentration that, were it not for the arrival of a fellow companion with the news of a communal gathering, they might well have remained in the garden for an even longer period of time.

"Come Hasan," Amin said, picking himself up. "There are others I want you to meet before you rest."

As a warm feeling welled up inside of him, Hasan joined his brother. "It is good to be with you again," he said, smiling. Turning together, the two men departed for the line of fluttering tents in the distance.

THE NEXT FEW DAYS brought to Hasan the realization that the differences among the followers of the Báb were not restricted to their understandings of his messianic claims. He learned that on a deeper level there were fundamental disagreements as to the nature and aim of the movement as a whole. To some it was a call to reform, a return to the purity of early Islam, while to others it was a revolutionary creed dedicated to loosing its followers from the shackles of the past. And between these two extremes were various shades of gray.

As his brother's speech had demonstrated, and each new day's activities further confirmed, Amin was a firm supporter of the revolutionary faction. But, though his youthful idealism was strong, he was not its leader. This position was reserved for a young poetess, Qurratu'l-'Ayn. By the force of her personality and the eloquence of her words, she had from the beginning of the conference championed the call to change. In a world dominated by men, she was blazing a path of her own, one which saw in the Báb's claims and teachings a trumpet blast that would usher in a new era. Her ideas, however, were not without opposition. Not only the conservatives, but those of more moderate bent, found themselves at odds with this dynamic female. Most prominent among the latter was one of the Báb's first disciples and his first lieutenant, Mullá Muḥammad-'Alí, known as Quddús. Throughout the Badasht meeting, Quddús had done his best to maintain unity. However, for the last several days he had been openly hostile toward the young woman. Now, as Hasan waited with his brother outside Quddús's tent, there was fear in the camp that the growing conflict might lead to a complete rupture.

"What are you going to say to him?" asked Hasan, trying to hide his anxiety.

"I want to discuss Qurratu'l-'Ayn's position," answered Amin, "since he will not see her and all communication has been broken off."

"Then you will act as her spokesman?"

"Not officially. She has not asked me to come here. But if we are to prevent a major split, there must be dialog. Quddús cannot allow himself to simply ignore what she is saying."

Hasan was about to respond to his brother's answer with another question when the flap of the tent abruptly flew open and a heavily bearded attendant invited them in. "My master will see you now," he announced.

Seconds later the two brothers were standing in front of the man on whose shoulders lay the weight of the moment. Robed entirely in black with a matching turban, his bearded face reflected a willfullness that knew no bounds. Hasan took his expression as a sign of arrogance. To Amin, who knew better, his glaring eyes and stony features were merely signs of his intense inner convictions.

Quddús directed his visitors to a brightly colored carpet in the middle of the tent. Politely waving away the attendant, he briefly adjusted his turban and then joined the two men, sitting down comfortably on his heels. "Salaam. May God shower his blessings upon you," he said without changing his facial expression.

"And may He continue to grant you the wisdom of a true believer," returned Amin.

"You have come on business?" asked the black-robed figure, brushing aside any further formalities. "Is it about Qurratu'l-'Ayn?"

"Yes." Amin braced himself for what he feared was to come.

"Do you support her position?"

"I feel that what she has to say is significant, and that she should not be prevented from expressing her views."

"Then you are acting as her envoy?"

"No, I have come of my own will."

Quddús did not reply. Instead he stared sullenly at his outspoken visitor. From where he was sitting, Hasan could see that Quddús was deeply locked in thought. Does he consider Amin too brash? the older brother pondered. Will he dismiss him as an insolent intruder?

"She is extreme in her opinions," said Quddús at last, breaking the silence. "She speaks as if she were the appointed representative of our Master."

"No doubt Qurratu'l-'Ayn is a forceful person," Amin began. "But like some of us, she feels that our Master's cause is diluted by those who do not have the courage to accept its implications."

"And I suppose you know what she is calling for?" The voice of Quddús became more challenging. "She demands that we rid ourselves of ablutions and the laws of purity—that we forget the fast of Ramadan, and ignore the holy days associated with the Imams—that we no longer face Mecca when we pray . . . In short, she is calling for the abolition of the *sharia,* the Holy Law of Islam."

"But has not Sayyid-i Báb claimed to be the Qá'im, the Lord of the Age? And does He not have the power to abrogate all laws?" shot back Amin in a tone which Hasan feared was too forceful.

"We are not sure of the exact nature of his latest claims," Quddús replied with some hesitation. "Until we know precisely what they mean, we cannot afford to move forward recklessly. We are already accused by the mullás of being devils and enemies of Islam. To introduce Qurratu'l-'Ayn's policies now would play into the hands of those who have made it their purpose to destroy us."

"Then you are saying that we should bow to the attacks of our opponents?" asked Amin increduously.

"My dear rebel," said Quddús, lowering his voice considerably. "I myself know that the Báb is not merely a spokesman for the Imam, and that He has the authority to do as He wishes. Qurratu'l-'Ayn is correct when she says that the *sharia* is a thing of the past, and our Lord—peace be upon Him—will no doubt gradually do away with most of it. But He has made no such changes as yet. Now is not the time. Our numbers are few, and we are surrounded by enemies. Your statements, and even those of

Qurratu'l-'Ayn are sound. But at this moment not all men are capable of receiving such knowledge. When the time has come, it will be made known to us. As for now, although a few are ready, we must be patient. To do otherwise would shatter the community beyond repair. You may tell her this.''

"So you will not meet with her?''

"I have made my position clear on several occasions. And I say again that if my leadership is accepted, and she comes to me, then I am willing to consult. But I refuse to go to her. Now I must take my leave. Peace be upon you both.''

The conversation having been bluntly concluded, Amin and Hasan quietly departed Quddús's quarters. To the younger man the meeting was an indication that the split in the Bábí camp was becoming increasingly unbridgeable. He could not help showing his disappointment. Hasan, on the other hand, not only continued to be amazed at the intensity with which each faction asserted its position, he found that his initial bewilderment concerning the real nature of the claims and message of the Báb had turned to utter confusion. Who is this man, he asked himself, that he can attract such a diverse group of followers? As to his own sentiments, Hasan sided with his brother: the hypocritical, corrupt society that encircled them had to be shaken to its core. But whether this was the sayyid's goal, or whether any religious movement could ever produce such a result, he did not know. And from what he had seen thus far, neither did the Bábís.

Chapter 7

"O FIRM ONES in the way of righteousness. There are those among us who say that the Qá'im cannot appear until certain conditions as made evident in the traditions have become manifest. Only when the prophecies have been literally fulfilled, they claim, can the Beloved of the Lord show Himself to the faithful."

The voice that carried these words was distinctly female, yet while the feminine tone rounded and softened the emanating syllables, it by no means diminished their evocative force. This was Qurratu'l-'Ayn's secret—her ability to unite feminine charm with the power of knowledge—and as the small group of men listened from the other side of the partition behind which custom forced her to speak, they could only look straight ahead in reverent awe.

The structure was not elaborate, merely a long canvas flap which had been taken from the tent's entryway and placed across one of its far corners. Held up on the ends by long pieces of wood driven into the ground, it stretched approximately ten feet from side to side and rose the same distance upward. In religious circles it was the equivalent to the veil, and on those rare occasions when women were given the opportunity to express their knowledge, it was a mandatory contraption.

"If these premises are examined closely," continued Qurratu'l-'Ayn, "it will be seen that they deny any possibility that the Qá'im will become manifest. What they have done is to relegate him to the oblivion of a never-ending future. In doing this, they have discarded the warning of such an eminent soul as the Imám Músá Kázim who, as tradition records, stated the following: 'On that day the ignorant shall be wise and the wise ignorant. Those who . . . ' ''

In the midst of her presentation, the discourse was interrupted. Bursting into the tent from a side entryway, a small, white-robed man panted out his message. ''Quddús has called an assembly. He requires that all of you attend.''

''All of us?'' the voice behind the curtain asked.

The man's lowered head and silent tongue revealed the answer.

''If you cannot attend, then we will not either,'' shouted Amín as he flew to his feet.

''Yes,'' confirmed another devotee, jumping up. ''We should not attend the meeting.''

The boisterous outcries which followed the men's statements indicated that the consensus in the room was one of support for their proposals. But the enthusiasm for rebellion was quickly extinguished by Qurratu'l-'Ayn herself. ''You must go,'' she said. ''Show Quddús the respect that he deserves.''

As an indication of the regard the men had for the young woman's authority, not one of them spoke a word of protest. Instead, they joined their two comrades on their feet and filed out behind Quddús's messenger.

The tent toward which the companions proceeded was on the opposite side of the encampment from that of Qurratu'l-'Ayn. Consequently, by the time they had made their way to its large, folded-flap doors there was hardly any room for them to enter. Only the far corner of the canvas structure remained unoccupied, and it was here that the latecomers were finally able to settle themselves.

The surrounding scene was one of calm and respose.

Despite the tension of the last few days, men of varying ideological persuasions sat peacefully together waiting for the meeting to begin. In their minds, of course, there was an edginess as they flirted with feelings of unresolved anxiety, but outwardly tranquility seemed to prevail.

In the corner, opposite Amin and Hasan, were the two figures who had planned the conclave. Seated above the others on a low divan which acted both as a resting seat and a bed, the two men conversed quietly with one another, their lips at times barely appearing to move. One, Ḥusayn-'Alí, was recovering from the illness that had confined him to his bed for the past few days. Robed in blue, he was in need of several bulky pillows to keep him upright. Still, despite his condition, he radiated a look of profound serenity. To anyone who could see the large brown eyes that sat like glowing embers above his full black beard, it was readily apparent why this nobleman's son had become a powerful force within the ranks of those who followed the Báb. Next to him sat Quddús, still projecting an image of utter seriousness.

"What do you think is going to happen?" said Hasan, leaning over and whispering into Amin's ear.

"Who knows? From the look on Quddús's face I would say that he hasn't changed his mind."

A stirring at the tent's entryway ended the brothers' conversation, and they turned to see what was causing the commotion. Seconds later, their questions were answered. A gray-robed, white-turbaned man broke free from the host of believers surrounding the entryway and burst fervently into the crowded room.

"Isn't that Mehdi Qazvini, Qurratu'l-'Ayn's messenger?" blurted out Hasan. "I thought he was with us."

Not wavering for an instant, the man approached the

divan and its two seated figures. His mission was obviously an important one, for he had not even reached his destination when he began to deliver the message with which he had been entrusted. "O Master Quddús," he said, bowing in mid-stride. "My mistress Qurratu'l-'Ayn requests that you visit her in her garden."

Quddús looked up as if he were expecting such a request and replied immediately. "You can tell your mistress that I have entirely severed myself from her. Not only do I refuse to go to her garden, I decline even to meet with her."

The messenger bowed again and departed, leaving behind him a room filled with conjecturing whispers. From one side of the tent to the other, Quddús's vehement response was discussed. "Why was he so hostile?" "Does this mean a complete split?" "What will the young poetess say?" As for the man whose words they were analyzing, he turned back toward the man in blue and continued his conversation as if nothing had happened.

In contrast to Quddús's composure, Amin was nearly beside himself with rage. "How can he be so uncompromising?" he exclaimed in a voice loud enough for all those sitting near to hear.

"She is the one who is uncompromising," shot back a man sitting behind him. "Quddús has shown more patience with her than I would have."

"That is because you are blind to her spiritual power," said Amin, turning around to meet his adversary eye to eye. "Neither you, nor those like you, have the courage she possesses."

Angered at Amin's cutting insult, the man reached down to his side. He seemed ready to remove a long-bladed dagger from inside his robe when another uproar at the back of the tent startled him and diverted his attention. Once again Mehdi Qazvini had returned. Just as he had done several minutes earlier, he was jostling his way through the crowd toward the Bábí leaders. Moving rapidly, his face flushed with emotion, he passed through the last group of believers and proudly stationed himself in front of the divan. "Qurratu'l-'Ayn insists on your visit," he announced.

Although he had heard him perfectly well, Quddús did not move an inch. Looking into the face of his blue-robed comrade, he pursued their discussion with even greater vigor—a slight which enfuriated the messenger and caused him to unsheath his sword. "I refuse to go without you," he yelled. Holding his weapon out from his body, he tossed it at the feet of the undaunted lieutenant. "Either choose to accompany me to the presence of my mistress or cut off my head."

With a look of rage, Quddús turned to the courier. For several moments he glared into the man's eyes, and then, in a voice that would have made a leopard cringe, he spoke his mind. "I have already declared my intention not to visit Qurratu'l-'Ayn. If you insist, then I am willing to comply with the alternative you have put before me."

As the astonished companions looked on, Mehdi Qazvini knelt and stretched out his neck to receive the fatal blow he had requested. Quddús, not wavering one moment from his resolve, reached down and picked up the sword. The rays of sunlight that squeezed through the small openings in the tent's top danced on the surface of the rising metal blade, making it appear as if it was some type of golden wand and the man in whose hands it rested a performing magician.

To a man, all held their breath as Quddús stopped the

upward movement of the sword and prepared for its descent. Then, as he was about to complete the deed, a shrill voice from the back of the tent drew his attention. "Wait!"

Turning around, the assembled men were met with a shock. There, standing in the entryway was the woman whose supplication had resulted in the scene they were now witnessing—and she was standing without her veil.

"Qurratu'l-'Ayn," gasped a number of the companions in unison. "She has lost her mind," yelled another. "Do not enter," cried still another. But rather than retire, the young woman boldly made her way through the crowd toward the front of the packed tent.

The picture she presented as she passed by the stunned followers was a strange mixture of courage and beauty. Upright in stature, her long, silky, black hair flowed down onto the brocaded shoulder patches of the green and gold gown she wore. She moved with a grace reserved for a saint or a phophet. Glistening ebony eyes and soft, olive-hued cheeks, which no man except her husband and closest of kin had ever seen, animated her presence. A furtive smile upon her dainty lips reflected an inner confidence. Such was her magnetism that, despite the fact that all around them men were hiding their faces in shame, both Amin and Hasan continued to gaze unabashed at her seemingly divine countenance.

When Qurratu'l-'Ayn reached the front of the tent, she stepped up to the divan and seated herself on the right hand side of Quddús. In contrast to her unruffled serenity, the audience she now faced was in a state of near panic. Some men hid their faces in their hands, or covered them with the edges of their robes. Others touched their heads to the floor, while many who had the courage to look into her beautiful eyes heaped insults on their owner for so boldly displaying them. To a person of less fortitude, such remonstrations would have caused an immediate departure, but Qurratu'l-'Ayn held her head high and remained steadfast in her resolve.

Finally, in a gesture of ultimate horror, a brown-robed man with a long, thin gray beard jumped to his feet. Raising his sword to his throat, he pulled the blade across his unprotected skin. A moment later, spurts of blood filled the air, staining not only the side of the man's face and the edge of his white turban, but covering those next to him with dark purple blotches. "She is a sorceress," he yelled. Dropping his sword, he turned and fled. From other parts of the tent, small groups of men also departed briskly, while others who may have wished to do so found themselves paralyzed by bewilderment.

To this point, Quddús had remained calm. Now, however, a terrifying look of anger returned to his face, and many who saw him feared that he might use the sword still resting in his hand to strike the woman. But Qurratu'l-'Ayn refused to be affected by his wrathful glance. She quashed any thought of action that he may have been considering by rising to her feet and addressing the remnant of the assembly.

The words that poured from her lips were as moving as any Amin had ever heard. Throughout the stirring speech, the young man could feel his own spiritual unity with the unveiled beauty. The thoughts she expressed were ones he knew were his also: the purpose of the new message was not just to reform Islam, neither was its founder merely a saint. This was a new day, and a new order was called for. Sayyid-i Báb, the Qá'im, had spoken, and the entire world had been revolutionized.

"Verily," she announced, throwing her head back, "amid gardens and rivers shall the pious dwell in the seat of Truth, in the presence of the potent King." Quickly glancing at Ḥusayn-'Alí, she concluded in a burst of eloquence: "I am the word which the Qá'im is to utter, the word which shall put to flight chiefs and nobles of the earth. This day is the day of festivity and rejoicing, the day on which the fetters of the past are burst asunder. Let those who have shared in this great achievement arise and embrace each other."

Qurratu'l-'Ayn's speech sent a shock wave throughout the tent. Everyone, regardless of his position, had to make a decision. Even Hasan, who had been only an observer until now, was jolted by the explosion. His heart pounded rapidly, sending gushing spurts of enthusiasm through his body. He had heard the renouned poetess speak before and was aware of her charismatic power, but this was different. No longer was it obscure words and theological references. No longer was it the reflection of an outmoded, clerical style of thinking. Here was action, bold action, and he was drawn to it as to a magnet. This was something he could believe in, an open attack on the system he had come to despise. Without need of reflection, he knew that he had cast his lot with the Bábís. Leaping up, he threw his right hand into the air and yelled at the top of his voice. *"Yá Ṣáḥibu'z Zamán!* Victory to the Lord of the Age!"

Chapter 8

THE DEEP ORANGE FLAMES of the small fire danced wildly in the evening breeze, slowly consuming the twisted pieces of brittle wood and sending faint puffs of chalky smoke spiraling upward into the darkness. Fire had always fascinated Hasan. It was as if the darting flashes of color had a power over him. Whenever he looked into their midst he became hypnotized. Such was the case now: the effect of his fixed gaze was a transposition in time. For the moment, he was no longer camped with his companions at the side of a country road near the village of Níyálá: he was back at Badasht. The words that were ringing in his ears were those of the Qur'an.

"When the inevitable day of judgment shall suddenly come,
no soul shall charge the prediction of its coming with falsehood:
it will abase some, and exalt others.
When the earth shall be shaken with a violent shock
and the mountains shall be dashed to pieces
and shall become as dust scattered abroad;
and ye shall be separated into three distinct classed:
the companions of the right hand,
and the companions of the left hand,
and those who have preceded others in the faith
shall precede them to paradise.
These are they who shall approach near unto God:
they shall dwell in the gardens of delight."

The voice which had sent this sacred verse echoing through the tent was that of the man in blue, Ḥusayn-'Alí. In the midst of the upheaval that Qurratu'l-'Ayn's appearance had produced, he had thrown his support behind the poetess. The power with which he had delivered his address had reconciled many to her earth-shattering act. Even Quddús, whose initial impulse had been to sever the blasphemous head from its gowned body, was won over. When the air finally cleared, there remained a smaller but more united body of believers. From now on, they would not see themselves as Muslims tied to the past, but as Bábís dedicated to the future.

"What do you think it is," asked Javad, breaking the silence and bringing Hasan back to the present, "that makes men cling to tradition? Why do the things of which His Holiness the Báb speaks cause them to become so agitated and react so violently?"

"It is the narrow-mindedness of the mullás," answered Ali. "Having lived with one, it is not hard for me to understand. They see themselves as the sole interpreters of God's will on earth. They do not trust men to make judgments for themselves. Investigation and reason are cast aside and replaced by so-called scholarly authority. In such a system the ordinary man is given no chance to exercise his own faculty of choice. He is made to think that anything different, any move toward change, is inherently evil and harmful to the condition of his soul."

"I think it is more than that," interjected Amin from his position at the base of a small tree. "All mullás are not that narrow. Rather, I believe that men develop a spiritual inertia that stifles their creativity. When they see this creative faculty freely expressed by others, they react with fear. Their hostility is only an expression of those inner fears."

"And what is it that they fear?" asked Javad.

"Nothingness. Without the comfort of their conditioned beliefs they would have to drain themselves, and this they cannot do. Most men want the security of knowing that they are right. They find this security in tradition and established authority."

Although Hasan found the discussion interesting, and was capable of making his own contribution, he was not in the mood for theorizing. His mind had shifted: all he could think about was the task the newly unified group had set for itself on departing Badasht. So instead of adding his own thoughts on the matter at hand, he ignored his brother's remarks. With a sudden volley of words, he changed the conversation's direction. "What do you think of our chances of success?"

To the men sitting around the fire the question was not entirely unexpected. During the time they had come to know Hasan they had learned many of his idiosyncrasies, not the least of which was a powerful tendency toward absorption. Amin knew it as a family trait: one Hasan shared with him, and with Nematullah as well. While the others did not have this insight, they nevertheless accepted it as part of the young man's personality, and without any sign of annoyance gave way to the unrelated query.

"The prison will be well guarded," answered Javad after several moments of reflection. "But with the advantage of surprise we should be able to free Him."

"It is said that Sayyid-i Báb has almost a mystic control over his jailers," added a man sitting next to Hasan. "We may not even have to raise a sword."

"I doubt that." Ali threw some twigs and leaves into the fire. "It will be a hazardous venture, at least."

"But one that is certainly necessary," said Amin. "The

Day of Judgment is at hand. We must do all we can to aid the Qá'im in his victory."

Suddenly, Hasan's thoughts were violently shaken by a cry from Javad. "What is that?" he yelled, pointing down the roadway.

Following the line of Javad's outstretched hand, the friends peered out into the darkness. Their eyes eventually came to rest on several small spheres of flickering light. "They look like torches," declared Amin.

"It must be the local villagers." Ali clambered to his feet. "I wonder what they could want?"

It was not long before they found out, for the party of men was moving rapidly toward them. In front were three mullás spitting out Quranic verses castigating infidels. Behind them, armed with a variety of weapons and excited by the screeching voices, marched at least two hundred villagers.

When the group came closer, one of the divines ordered the villagers to stop. Stepping forward, he disclosed their purpose. "Do not defile our village with your presence," he shouted. "May the wrath of God fall upon you if you do not immediately depart."

"And may the Qá'im find you wanting on the Day of Judgment," yelled back a defiant Javad.

Such a display of disdain was all the provocation the mullá needed. Holding the flaring torch aloft, he pointed it in the direction of the companions. In a voice that resembled a cavalry commander's, he yelled at the top of his lungs. "*Alláh-u Akbar.*"

The mob reacted. From all sides of the angered mass of humanity, rocks were flung. Those who carried other weapons—sticks, straps, and, in some cases, knives—raised them menacingly above their heads, all the while filling the air with the foulest of curses and insults. Slowly the front rows edged forward.

By this time the friends were not alone. Other Bábís from nearby campfires had heard the commotion and joined them. But the advantage of numbers still lay with the villagers. Realizing that any confrontation could only be damaging to their cause, the Bábís scurried to their horses.

Seeing the prey flee, the villagers halted their advance. However, if their movement had stopped, the volume of their voices increased. Encircled by the light of the bright swaying torches, they sang out in spontaneous unison. The message they left with the dispersing Bábís was a warning of things to come: "Death to all infidels. Death to Sayyid-i Báb. Death to all infidels. Death to Sayyid-i Báb."

Chapter 9

HASAN LOOKED OUT over the fortifications at the landscape below. Except for a few isolated clumps of trees, sage brush prevailed; and the constant pounding it had taken over the past few weeks had reduced much of that wiry vegetation to mere roots. To the north and east of the newly constructed fort, rolling hills predominated, while to the south the desolate scene gradually gave way to green forests and undulating mountains.

As he scanned the horizon, Hasan could see scattered clouds of dust, a sign that the government troops were once again making ready for action. How utterly absurd, he thought, that in this remote land, far from the centers of power, the shah's vizier had assembled an entire army to pursue a few hundred Bábís. Nevertheless, the troops were present, and it appeared they would not leave until they had accomplished the task they had been sent to perform.

Hasan turned away from the view before him and climbed down from the platform behind the fortifications. Hitting the ground with a thud, he turned to see Amin, who greeted him with a question. "Could you see anything?"

"They are preparing for something," replied Hasan. "I was on my way to inform Quddús."

As he spoke, Hasan reflected on Amin's obvious youth. The fullness of his beardless face, the smoothness of his skin, his wavy black hair, and his round sparkling eyes all confirmed this fact. Too young to die, he thought. Too young to die.

Hasan left Amin and headed toward the far end of the

compound. His destination was a small battered building, the shrine to a local saint named Shaykh Ṭabarsí, which the beseiged believers had turned into a military headquarters. Moving through the grounds, he passed men at work: some sharpening swords, others cleaning equipment, and still others grooming horses. They had been here four months now and were used to such work: they found no difficulty in raising their heads to briefly converse with Hasan as they went on with their duties.

When the disciples had fled from the mob of angry Níyálá villagers, they had split up into smaller groups. Some had journeyed to Mashhad to join Mullá Ḥusayn, one of the Báb's chief lieutenants, who had been directed by his imprisoned Master to unfurl a black flag, the symbol of the awaited Qá'im. Others had dispersed to the various cities of Khurasan. But their escape was to bring them no peace. Those, including Amin and Hasan, who had enrolled under the black standard were soon attacked again—this time near the town of Bárfurúsh. Defending themselves, the company took to arms and drove their attackers away, securing thereby a temporary truce. But as they left the town, they were ambushed by troops under the provincial military commander and subsequently driven onto the grounds of the shrine which had now become their fortress. Thus was the small band transformed by circumstance into a permanently armed troop.

On reaching the shrine, Hasan called out for permission to enter. Once given leave to proceed, he pushed open the metal-studded wooden door and entered a small room, a onetime alcove to the main sanctuary. In one corner of the dusty cubicle lay the fragments of rubble that had fallen from the roof. On the opposite side stood the fraying black standard. Between them, his back leaning against the dirt-covered wall, sat Quddús, whose bloodstained and torn cloak evidenced the struggle in which they were involved. He was busy studying a map when Hasan came in.

"What news?" Quddús asked, looking up.

"There is movement in their camp."

"An attack?"

"I cannot say. But they are definitely preparing for something."

Quddús folded his hands and glanced at the black standard. "Mullá Husayn will lead a sortie at dawn," he announced. "Pass the word."

Hasan saluted and left the room. Once more in the sunlight, he hurried across the compound, informing men, as he went, of the order he had just received. Ten minutes later he was back with his brother, who by this time had been joined by Ali. "We will attack at dawn," he told them. "You should both get some rest."

The two men nodded in agreement and sat down at the base of the protective wall which they had just helped to construct. Meanwhile, Hasan climbed back up to the viewing platform to take one last look at the horizon. Seconds later he was on the ground again preparing a headrest with his saddle and blanket. Then he sat down, stretched out his legs, leaned his head against the saddle, and closed his eyes.

Dreamily, Hasan considered the events of the past few months. The concluding days at Badasht had stirred him deeply. For the first time in his life he had been uplifted by the spirit of faith, and his following meeting with Mullá Husayn had further strengthened his resolve. Almost immediately that faith had been tested—the various assaults, his killing of an attacking mullá at Bárfurúsh, followed by the strenuous flight from the town and the hurried arrival at the shrine. It had all happened so fast.

Too fast. For the last three months, the continual attacks of the government troops. Only the wisdom of Mullá Ḥusayn, who had the insight to procure supplies and to build a protective wall around the shrine, had saved them —and even then it seemed they were only buying time. Perhaps he should have listened to Nematullah.

Slowly Hasan's thoughts became less clear. Soon they were only traces, dangling, darting, disappearing. From the back of his throat came a slow and rhythmic gargle; he was asleep.

Ali looked over at Amin, who like himself was unable to sleep. "Are you afraid?" he whispered.

"No," said Amin. "I just don't like waiting. The time seems to go by so slowly."

Momentarily Ali allowed the silence that had followed Amin's response to remain, then hesitantly he again addressed his companion. "It is hard to accept that Javad is no longer with us. He was so vibrant and enthusiastic."

"Yes," said Amin. "But your faith is being tested. You must look at Javad's death as a sacrifice—an oblation— to the birth of a new Faith."

"Yes, I know my faith is not all it should be."

"That is because you have not learned to put complete confidence in God," continued Amin eagerly. "In that way you are like Hasan. Your mind interferes with your soul."

Again there was a period of quiet as Ali digested the words he had just heard. They showed much insight into his nature, as if Amin were his own brother. And yet Amin was still a stranger. True, Ali had confided in him, revealing his episode with Shahin. But even then it was the young man's mysterious power of attraction, rather than true friendship, that had caused Ali to unveil his soul. It was as if a psychic magnetism had compelled him to open his innermost being; and that power was once again pulling him to confession. "Amin, do you recall the talk we had several days ago?" he began.

"Of course."

"At that time I told you about my experience in my uncle's mosque and how I felt when I heard you speak at Badasht. But I did not mention the fact that I still have fears."

"Of what sort?"

"I realize it sounds strange, but sometimes—almost out of nowhere—the feeling comes to me that I have not been forgiven. I still see images of Shahin and her husband. They taunt me, they accuse me, and I become helpless—paralyzed."

"From what you say," Amin broke in, "your problem seems to be your own polytheism."

"What?" Ali was aghast at what he had just heard.

"Don't take me wrong, my friend. I do not mean to criticize you. What I have said is related to my earlier comment. You seem more concerned with the judgment of men than you are with the judgment of God. This lack of faith is, in the truest sense, what the Qur'an refers to as polytheism—putting something other than God before Him."

"I understand what you are saying, Amin. And no doubt there is some truth in your observation. However, it is not just a matter of fearing the judgment of men: it is the problem of justice. My conscience tells me that somehow I should have to pay for what I have done."

"But haven't you paid? Hasn't the agony of your guilt been sufficient retribution?"

"That, I do not know. At times I feel that is so. Then I

think of the suffering I have caused and wonder how I could possibly be forgiven.''

Amin looked closely at his new friend and saw in his eyes a tortured anguish that generated within him a genuine feeling of pity. As with Hasan, he wanted to reach out and give Ali his own faith. Yet he knew that this was impossible. All he had was the power of the spoken word. He gripped both his friend's shoulders urgently, looking directly into his eyes. "There are three things I want to say to you, my dear Ali. First, God has forgiven you. This is apparent from your experience in the mosque. It is you who have not forgiven yourself. Second, even though you may have hurt others, you cannot change the past. What is done, is done. No amount of suffering on your part will change that. What is more, the pain you may have caused others is limited; like yourself, they can always turn to God for their healing. Third, and to my mind most important, you seem to have been influenced by your uncle more than you realize. From what you have told me, he was completely legalistic in his approach to religion. Such an approach leaves no room for mercy and compassion. It always rests on the surface of life, unable to penetrate to the tragic dimensions of existence. It is primarily concerned with punishment. It bypasses love; and although it speaks of justice, it is based on revenge. It offers no healing, no transfiguration of the soul. It is sterile and cold, and its God becomes the culmination of all man's pettiness and spite.

"I ask you, is this the God of our ancestors?" Amin became more excited as he went on. "Is this the God that the Prophet Muḥammad—peace be upon him—invoked before every sura of the Qur'an as the All-Merciful, the All-Compassionate? Is this the God whom our beloved

Báb has hailed as the uncompromising lover of mankind? I say not.

"Do not allow yourself to become a follower of this idol. Trust in Him whose love and compassion the most holy of saints have not been able to fathom. As for those who deny Him, whether it be in the name of equity or justice, leave them to themselves. For those who have not been in need of his love will not see Him." With these words Amin released his grip and leaned back against the wall, closing his eyes.

Ali, however, could not sleep as he meditated on the things that Amin had said.

Slowly the time passed. Gradually the heat of mid-afternoon began to subside, and across the compound long shadows started to appear. But despite the indications that evening would soon be upon them, the beseiged men continued to sleep. Except for the guards, only Ali remained awake, his mind unable to unleash itself from the earlier conversation. Looking up, he watched the slow movement of the clouds that had gathered on the horizon. "We will certainly need your help," he whispered to them.

For another four hours, the men of Fort Ṭabarsí continued to rest. Finally, starting at the area closest to the shrine and slowly radiating outward like ripples on a disturbed pond, the camp came to life. Still weary, the men started to make preparations for the approaching battle: readying equipment, nourishing their bodies, and saying prayers.

By the time the stirrings had reached the outer wall, Ali had roused Amin and Hasan. The three companions had just started to gather their belongings, when a rising of voices from the middle of the compound drew their attention. Mullá Ḥusayn had made his appearance.

Of medium height and frail of form, Quddús's appointed commander for the morning's sortie was wearing what the torch-lit night revealed to be a freshly prepared brown robe. Beneath the garment protruded small, square shoulders which were held back with the utmost dignity. Above his narrow brow sat a green turban, a treasured gift from his incarcerated Master. Strapped to his side was a sword of such size and weight that it might have more properly belonged to a man of much bigger stature.

The appearance of Mullá Husayn set in motion a small-scale pilgrimage. From all parts of the compound, men stopped what they were doing and made their way toward him. Following the surge to the shrine, Amin, Hasan, and Ali joined the large circle that surrounded the venerable leader, waiting for his command.

A slowly raised hand was all that Mullá Husayn needed to enjoin silence. "Believers in the Cause of God," he began. "It has been one hundred and sixteen days now since we took refuge at this shrine. During this time, all of you have exemplified that inordinate courage which comes from unwavering faith. Rest assured that the sacrifices you and your fallen comrades have made will not go unrewarded. You are the vanguard of a new race of men. Future generations will look back at your extraordinary deeds and glorify them with words of unrestricted praise. It was you, amongst all the men of your time, who heeded the call of God. I say to you now, that this act shall never be forgotten."

Choked with emotion, Mullá Husayn paused. Once again regaining his composure, he continued to address his troops. "During the past few days it has become ever more apparent to Quddús and myself that we cannot hold out much longer against the constant onslaught of the government troops. I am sure that you are all aware of our situation. Supplies are extremely low. Therefore, as you have been informed, we have decided to attack the enemy tonight, just before the sun rises. Let those who wish to join me be ready to issue forth from behind these walls to scatter once again the dark forces which have beset our path, and ascend to the heights of glory. We will depart when the morning star appears.''

A silent bow of the head indicated that Mullá Ḥusayn had finished his speech. Quickly turning around, the green-turbaned commander made his way through the crowd. As if following a choreographed sequence, one after another the men began to peel back, each bowing his head in reverence as the man who would shortly lead them into battle swept by and disappeared into the interior of the shrine.

IN THE EARLY HOURS of the new day, when the morning star had just slipped above the horizon, Mullá Ḥusayn appeared at the door of the shrine. This time the men were ready for him. With their swords firmly attached to their belts, they anxiously awaited his signal. As he strode to his horse, the commander glanced up at the morning star, his lips twitching in silent prayer. Mounting his horse, he waved his sword skyward, and the three hundred and thirteen men under his charge threw themselves upon their animals and followed him through the open gates and onto the surrounding plain.

As quietly as they could, the men of Fort Ṭabarsí marched toward the first barricade of the enemy line. Even though the clouds had not come to help them, this was the safest part of the mission, as the darkness hid them from their foe. Still, each member of the party did his best to ensure that neither man nor beast made any unnecessary noise.

If we can only catch them by surprise, Hasan thought. If they know we are coming, it could be a disaster.

When the troop was only two hundred yards away from the first barricade, the men spread out into two long lines. By the time this maneuver had been completed, the distance between them and their enemy had been halved. Hasan felt the mounting anxiety as a tightening in his throat. Just a few seconds more and . . .

The tension was broken. Raising his sword above his head, Mullá Ḥusayn pushed his heels into his horse's flanks and let out a cry. "*Yá Ṣáḥibu'z-Zamán!* O Lord of the Age!"

The Bábís charged. In seconds they had reached the enemy barricade. Unprepared for the assault, the government troops, many of them still rising from their beds, rushed for their weapons. Meanwhile, the men of Fort Ṭabarsí, their polished swords reflecting the rays of the breaking dawn, unleashed on them the full fury of their attack. Riding next to each other, Amin and Hasan eagerly displayed their new military skills, slashing one enemy soldier after another to the ground. Even Ali, who before the sojourn east had never held a sword, was now wielding his weapon as if he had been raised with it.

While the Bábís routed their opponents, Mullá Ḥusayn sought out the commander of the fleeing unit. Arriving at his tent, he overpowered the lone sentinel and drove the half-dressed officer onto the field of battle, finally dispatching him with one mighty swing of his sword. Wheeling his horse around, Mullá Ḥusayn pointed his blood-covered blade in the direction of the second barricade and galloped off. Following his leader's example, Hasan rallied the warriors around him, and with an eager cry led the enthusiastic horsemen in rapid pursuit of the green turban.

Although the soldiers at the second barricade had heard the uproar and were therefore better prepared for an attack, their fate was much the same as those who had manned the first line of defense. Despite the bullets which now whistled past on all sides of them, Mullá Ḥusayn's cavalry continued to fight like men possessed. But the royal troops, many of them raw recruits, found flight a more inviting prospect than the wrath of their assailant's swords.

After the initial resistance had given way, the Bábís took complete control. Those of their enemy who had not been able to escape found themselves either helplessly throwing their hands into the air or pursued by flaying sabers.

In a similar manner, the remaining three barricades fell to the unrelenting onslaught. In each case, the picture was the same: slashing swords; rearing, wide-eyed horses; fleeing, disoriented men; painful, death-filled groans. Although the number of dead and wounded among the Bábís increased with the winning of each new objective, when they had penetrated the last outpost, it was apparent that they had accomplished their mission.

As the last of the government troops began to flee, Hasan stopped to look for Amin. He had not seen his brother since leaving the previous barricade. Nowhere was Amin's familiar outline to be seen. Where could he be? he thought. And then, praying that it was the partial darkness of the early morning that concealed him, Hasan ended his search and rode off to join Mullá Ḥusayn, who was exhorting his troops to final victory.

As he waved his sword above his head, the Bábí leader was so absorbed in his task that he had not noticed his horse coming perilously close to the ropes of an enemy tent. By the time he became aware of the predicament, his wildly prancing steed had become entangled. Virtually suspended in midair, the commander tried to calm the animal, but in the middle of this distraction a shot rang out from a nearby tree. Hasan saw Mullá Ḥusayn grab his chest.

As two young men rushed forward to help him, Mullá Ḥusayn dismounted. Bleeding profusely, he staggered a few steps forward before falling heavily to the earth. Seconds later, the Bábís were at his side, ministering as best they could to their fallen chief. Hasan, meanwhile, dashed up and down the line of the barricade, sounding the retreat. With military precision, the warriors answered the call by immediately lowering their swords, allowing the last vestiges of the government troops to flee unopposed. They then gathered around their wounded commander and returned to the safety of Fort Ṭabarsí.

Chapter 10

THE SUN ROSE on a somber Fort. Painfully, the fatigued and hungry men rose from their places of rest to begin another day of waiting. Three months had elapsed since the forces of Mullá Ḥusayn had ventured forth and ravaged the barricades of the enemy. Although they had been victorious in their mission, and the government troops had been forced to abandon their immediate positions, the enemy had not been driven away altogether. With their return, the fort was once again under seige. Now, each passing day brought with it increased suffering.

Only hours after the Bábís' triumphant return to Fort Ṭabarsí, Mullá Ḥusayn had died from the gunshot wound he had received earlier that morning. His last few minutes were spent alone with Quddús. Upon Mullá Ḥusayn's passing, the new commander had clothed him in his own shirt and seen to it that he was laid to rest near the shrine in which he had taken his last breath. In a similar manner, the bodies of the thirty-six warriors who had also fallen were interred in a single grave. The words of Quddús sealed their common tomb: "Let the loved ones of God take heed of the example of these martyrs of our Faith. Let them in life be and remain united as these are now in death."

While the loss of Mullá Ḥusayn was a staggering blow to the weary men left behind, his untimely demise only marked the beginning of their agony. Although only thirty-six from among the three hundred and thirteen men who had left the fort on that memorable day had been killed, some ninety had been injured and most of these died of their wounds.

And then there were the conditions inside the fortress. A continual cold hovered over the region, causing both man and beast constant discomfort. With only the blankets of their horses to cover them, the men shivered through long, frigid nights. Even during the daylight hours they found little relief from the chilling winds that swept down on them from the mountains. Despite severe rationing, the last bags of stored rice had been consumed. Soon the men had no choice but to eat the flesh of their animals. The only variety offered to his forced diet was boiled grass and the leather from their saddles. In some cases, even the ground-up bones of the defleshed horses had been devoured.

Hasan sat perched on the same viewing platform that he had manned since his arrival at the fort. As he scanned the bleak horizon, he could see no sign of human movement. Only the new barricades, their boards covered with a thin layer of frost, were visible; not even the cannons which had been bombarding them for the past few weeks were in sight. When would they attack again? he asked himself. Even if the government troops greatly outnumbered them, a straightforward fight would be better than the endless waiting and the ever-increasing pain of hunger.

Hasan lowered his eyes and glanced at Amin, who was leaning against the base of the wall. How strange hope is, Hasan thought. Momentarily his mind returned to the day of the attack. Unable to locate his brother on the field of battle, he had hoped that he would find Amin safe and well at the fort. When he indeed found him in such a condition, he had been overcome with joy. But now, as he thought back, he knew that he must have realized that their situation was hopeless. Although the victory meant that they might survive another month or two, it was certainly only a matter of time before the inevitable happened. Yet, that afternoon none of those things seemed to matter. Amin was alive, and somehow that was all that was important.

As Hasan contemplated, Ali arrived and sat down next to Amin. He too had survived the attack, receiving only a minor leg wound which had healed. His horse, however, had not fared so well. Even though she lived, the last few weeks, without much more than a few handfuls of grass, had greatly weakened her. Now she was near death, and Ali had just returned from her side.

"How is she?" asked Amin.

"It doesn't look good."

"We need food today," ventured Hasan, hoping that his statement would not be taken as callous. "Perhaps you should put the poor creature out of her misery."

Ali took a deep breath and looked up at his friend. "Yes, you are right," he sighed. "It's just that it is hard."

"Would it help if I did it for you?" asked Hasan. "I have had to kill horses before."

"No." Ali continued to stare upward. "I will do it. I just need some time."

"Possibly she is the lucky one," said Hasan, trying to soften the blow. "God only knows what the next few days will be like: no food, little water."

"Do you think you can say you believe and not be tested?" said Amin suddenly.

Hasan looked angrily at his younger brother but did not respond. Instead he thought: just like Amin—unwavering in his belief, sometimes painfully so. Yet there was little doubt that such belief was a valuable asset. What was needed more than anything else in circumstances like these was unwavering faith.

"I will be back shortly," announced Ali, jumping to his feet and interrupting Hasan's train of thought. "It has to be done."

As Ali headed toward his grim task, Hasan watched him with the penetrating eyes of a sage. At that moment, he saw in his friend the perplexing human condition—vulnerable belief, assailed by the absurdities of suffering and evil, yet held together by a simple sense of duty.

While Hasan silently mused, Amin climbed up next to him and looked out over the sweeping plain. As his brother had done minutes earlier, he strained to find any sign of movement. There was nothing except the sterile barricades. Agitated at his discovery, he started to return to the ground, when out of the corner of his eye he caught sight of a swirl of dust. Concentrating his gaze on the rising cloud, he could just make out the figures of several horsemen. "Hasan, look!"

Hasan whirled around, startled by his brother's cry. "What is it?"

"Look out there!" Amin pointed toward the horizon. "Can you see them?"

It was several seconds before he saw them: three men on horseback cantering toward the fort.

"Can you make out who they are?" asked Amin.

"It looks like the dark gray of government troops."

"I wonder what they could be up to?"

"I don't know, but we'd better tell Quddús. Wait here."

Jumping down, Hasan had only taken his first few steps toward the shrine when he again heard the sound of Amin's shout. "Hasan, wait! They are carrying a book."

Hasan stopped and ran back toward the wall. Hoisting

himself up, he again looked out at the approaching visitors. They were much closer now, three distinct figures bouncing atop their loping horses. Just as Amin had said, one of them was holding a huge book high above his head.

When the horsemen were only several hundred yards from the fort, they pulled up their steeds and stopped. Almost simultaneously the man with the book began to wave it back and forth in front of his face. Observing the gesture, Hasan leaned over, and in an excited but controlled voice said, "It is a Qur'an. They want to talk. Keep an eye on them."

Hasan leaped to the ground and headed toward the shrine, while Amin kept a constant watch on the horsemen. Periodically, the man with the Qur'an would cease his waving motion, and lower the book. Then after several moments he would begin again. What could they possibly want? thought Amin. Why should they be asking for a meeting?

When Hasan finally arrived at his destination, he found Quddús applying cloths to the leg of a wounded comrade who had ventured out the previous day in search of food. Without the usual polite formalities, and short of breath, he divulged his information. "Outside the fort . . . government troops . . . carrying a Qur'an."

"What?" Quddús looked up from his work. "Did you say a Qur'an?"

"It appears that they want to talk," said Hasan. "They have stopped just a few hundred yards from the fortifications."

Quddús finished wrapping the man's leg and stood up to face the still panting Hasan. "What do you think?" he asked.

Surprised that Quddús would seek his opinion, Hasan

stood still momentarily before boldly airing his judgment. "What can we lose by talking to them?"

Quddús placed his hand on his bearded chin. After several seconds he again looked at Hasan. "You say there are three of them. Then get two company commanders and meet me at the gate in ten minutes."

Almost as soon as Quddús had finished his last words, Hasan hastened across the compound. The presence of the government troops was now common knowledge to the inhabitants of Fort Ṭabarsí, and thus he found no trouble locating Ṣadiq and 'Abu'l-Qasim, who were engaged in discussion with a large contingent of men. Breaking in on the conversation, he gave the two commanders their orders and then went to saddle his own mount.

Ten minutes later the three had assembled in front of the fortress gate. They were met by Quddús, who had emerged from the shrine to give them their final instructions, a duty he carried out with his usual speed and efficiency. Their orders understood, the Bábís acknowledged the commander with a brief salute and, pulling their horses around, rode through the gate and toward the waiting horsemen.

Once outside the fortress, Hasan could only think of the orders Quddús had conveyed: to stop twenty yards from the party; to approach only the group's commanding officer; not to be drawn any farther away from the fort; and to invite them inside for further consultation only if the soldiers surrendered their weapons. Hasan ran these steps through his mind. By the time they were within twenty yards of the government horsemen, he knew them as if he had been their creator.

Hasan inspected the gray-clad figures sitting impassively before him. Their red shoulder crests and dress sabers indicated that they were all officers, while one of them wore the insignia of a lieutenant. Their intentions seemed peaceful, as each man's rifle was firmly lodged in the carrying case at the side of its owner's saddle.

"We have seen your Qur'an," shouted Hasan after verifying his speculations with a quick glance at the book's gold ornamentation. "The peace of God and His Prophet be upon you. What do you want to say to us?"

The lieutenant, a dark man with broad shoulders and a powerful voice, answered: "We have come to make you an offer. We would like to speak to your commander."

Remembering Quddús's words, Hasan scrutinized the speaker. "If you want to enter the fortress you must surrender your weapons," he said finally in a loud commanding burst. "If you accept our conditions, throw down your rifles and swords in front of you."

Momentarily the lieutenant wavered, but after a few seconds, he ordered his fellow officers to follow Hasan's directions. The men removed their weapons from their holders and threw them down on the dry, sandy ground, forming as they did a rough pile of steel and wood to which the lieutenant himself added the last components. The process completed, Hasan signaled to his comrades to collect the hardware, and the two men jumped from their horses to carry out his orders.

As Hasan waited for them to remove the weapons, he felt an urge to ask the lieutenant exactly what his offer was. But knowing it was not his place to interrogate the officer, he remained silent and waited for Sadiq and 'Abu'l-Qasim to return to their horses. When they had done so, he gestured to the lieutenant to lead the way.

Minutes later, the train entered through the battered gateway of Fort Ṭabarsí, the weaponless soldiers in front and the Bábís behind. Maintaining this formation for the remainder of the short trip across the compound, the men arrived at the shrine and dismounted. The Bábí escorts stood aside. Again making their visitors lead the way, they followed them inside where they were met by the seated Quddús.

The black-turbaned leader did not speak. Instead, he leaned back, waiting.

"Your honored commander," began the officer with a phrase which Hasan at once recognized as a mere convention. "Our commander, Prince Mihdí Qulí, requests that two representatives be delegated to come to his camp and negotiate a peaceful end to this conflict." From the officer's tone of voice, it was clear he had memorized his lines.

"He wants us to come to him?" asked Quddús.

"He wants you to meet him in his own tent."

For over a minute Quddús did not speak, while the officer became increasingly restless. Finally, finding the extended quiet unbearable, the lieutenant interjected his own words of assurance. "I will personally guarantee your men's safe return."

After another brief lull, Quddús rose to his feet and instructed two men standing behind him to accompany the lieutenant. "Inform the prince," he said, "of our readiness to put an end to this struggle." Following a brief exchange of formalities, he dismissed them.

When the room was clear, Hasan, who had been watching the proceedings from the far corner, turned to Quddús. "Do you think they will be safe?" he asked.

"God will protect them," came the commander's quick reply. "We have nothing to fear."

As the delegates mounted their horses and prepared to leave the fortress, Hasan hurried back to his position on the far wall. Meanwhile, throughout the compound men gathered into small groups to speculate on what had happened inside the shrine. Where were their companions going? Was a truce at hand? Would they finally be allowed to leave Ṭabarsí? . . . Similar thoughts occupied the minds of Amin and Ali. As Hasan approached, they were quick to unleash a series of questions, which he answered with all the detail he could remember.

After he had explained what he had seen and heard, Hasan sat down and eyed the pieces of flesh that were waiting to be roasted on the small fire next to him. Ali's horse, he thought. Looking up at his companion, he realized how difficult it must have been for him to kill the mare.

Ali sensed the awkwardness of the moment and broke the tension. "It's certianly not a lamb pilaf."

"Compared to the bonemeal gruel we have had for the past few days, it seems like a delicacy," said Hasan. "Where is the rest of the meat? Did you distribute it?"

"She didn't have much left on her, and what there was didn't go very far."

"You can give my share to someone else," announced Amin. "I no longer feel any hunger."

"It is important that you eat, Amin," Hasan said. "You may well need the energy."

Amin's answer was silence, and Hasan knew that no amount of persuasion would change his mind. Accordingly, he did not pursue the issue any further but sat quietly watching the horseflesh slowly roasting on the fire.

A POUNDING SOUND in the distance started the half-conscious Hasan. Scrambling up to the platform, he looked down to see Quddús's ambassadors speeding toward the fort at full gallop. "They are back!" he cried.

By the time Hasan, Amin, and Ali arrived at the gate, the riders had already passed by the crowd that had gathered to meet them and were making their way across the dusty compound toward the shrine. Behind them surged the mass of Bábís, whose loud talk and wild gestulation created a scene which the trailing Hasan could only compare to a swarming nest of hornets.

Hasan joined the noisy throng just as the delegates were entering the shrine. Before the men had disappeared from sight, he noticed that one of them was carrying in his hands the same Qur'an that had been used earlier as a sign of truce. Hasan pointed to the volume. Why have they brought the Holy Book with them? he wondered.

Inside the shrine, Quddús was thinking the same thing. But rather than directly ask his comrade about the object now tucked under his arm, he spoke of that which most concerned him. "And what has the prince to say, Yúsuf?"

Mullá Yúsuf answered by placing the book before his commander and pointing to its opening page. There in the margin, in bold lettering, was the prince's handwritten message. Quddús lifted the Qur'án and began to read:

I swear by this most Holy Book, by the righteousness of God who has revealed it, and the Mission of Him who was inspired with its verses, that I cherish no other purpose than to promote peace and friendliness between us. Come forth from your stronghold and rest assured that no hand will be stretched forth against you. You yourself and your companions, I solemnly declare, are under the sheltering protection of the Almighty, of Muḥammad, His Prophet, and of Náṣiri'd-Dín Sẖáh, our sovereign. I pledge my honor that no man, either in this army or in this neighborhood, will ever attempt to assail you. The malediction of God, the omnipotent Avenger, rest upon me if in my heart I cherish any other desire than that which I have stated.

Quddús stared at the page. "He has affixed his personal seal."

"I saw him apply it with my own eyes," said Mullá Yúsuf. "Moreover, he has promised to send us a number of horses this very afternoon so that we may ride to the neighborhood of his camp. He will have a special tent raised for our reception."

"I still don't trust him," said the second delegate. "Why should a wolf allow its trapped victim to go free? It doesn't make sense."

Quddús paused for several thought-filled seconds and then raised the Holy Book heavenwards. "O Lord," he cried, "decide between us and between our people with truth; for the best to decide art Thou."

Quddús stood rigid, his arms stretched upward, as if waiting for an answer to his appeal. In like manner, his two comrades stood reverently still, anticipating the results of his prayer. Finally, the spell-like atmosphere was broken: Quddús lowered the book to his side, closed its pages, and started toward the door to inform the gathered companions of his decision.

The meeting spot just outside the door was packed with inquisitive men. They were all there, even the wounded. The sounds that filled the air around them reflected a mixture of hope and anxiety. Amid this din, Quddús lifted his right hand purposefully into the air until the noise subsided.

"My fellow believers in the Cause of God!" His voice reverberated through the now silent compound. "The

102

commander of our opponents, Prince Mihdí Qulí, has sent to us an offer. He says that he is willing to let us leave in peace if we will abandon our fortress and cease all hostilities. As an indication of his good intent, he has sent us a copy of the Holy Qur'an on which he has written his personal pledge. Therefore, as your commander I ask you to prepare yourselves to depart, for by our response to their invitation we shall enable them to demonstrate the sincerity of their intentions.''

When he was finished, Quddús raised the book and, putting his lips to the holy script, placed his own seal on the compact. His resolve thus signified, he pivoted around to quickly reenter the shrine, while the men dispersed to prepare for their journey to freedom.

Chapter 11

THE THREE COMRADES WATCHED the distant sky as the fires of the enemy camp sent clouds of smoke billowing upward. Although none of them said so, the brownish haze brought back childhood memories of the early-morning Shiraz horizon. They would have continued in their reminiscences had not Abdu'llah arrived suddenly and disturbed their thoughts. "And what do you think of the situation, my dear friends?"

"I don't like it," said Hasan. The prince has already violated one promise by not coming here. What should prevent him from committing further transgressions?"

"I agree with you," said Ali. "The prince is not a man of his word. He is not to be trusted."

"Quddús knows what is happening." Amin's voice was full of assurance. "Why do you think he wore the green turban when he left the fort?"

The event to which Amin was referring had taken place only a few hours after Quddús had addressed his comrades and pledged himself to accept the prince's oath. The promised horses had arrived and the commander appeared at the door of the shrine adorned in the headdress which, like the slain Mullá Ḥusayn, he had received as a gift from his beloved Master. Full of dignity and serenity, he had mounted the steed sent for him, and with his men trailing behind, some on horseback and others on foot, he had led them from their fortress to the tents and lodgings they now occupied.

Their new residence was located several miles from the

shrine that had sheltered them for the past seven months. A short distance from a small village, it overlooked the government camp and provided many of the men with the first full meal they had eaten in weeks. Still, despite the end of hostilities and the promise of freedom, a feeling of nervous mistrust pervaded the makeshift encampment. With each passing hour, that mistrust became more acute.

Several miles away, these fears were being confirmed. Early that morning Quddús had received a request from the prince to meet him at the royal headquarters. Accompanied by several attendants, he had left on horseback and journeyed to the government camp. However, upon arriving at the arranged meeting place, he was informed by the chief lictor that he would have to wait until noon to see the prince. But Mullá Yúsuf, who had accompanied Quddús was taken away and privately instructed by the prince's attendants to return at once to his camp and inform the Bábís that it was their leader's desire that they immediately disarm. Appearing to agree with the command, Mullá Yúsuf allowed the prince's lieutenants to escort him away from the headquarters, but just as he was to leave them he declared his own mistrust and galloped off.

The accompanying government troops reacted to this insolence with uncontrolled rage. Kicking their horses, they set out in pursuit of the fleeing Mullá Yúsuf. After a short chase they ran him down. Minutes later he was little more than a pulp-covered torso.

Their lust for action whetted, the soldiers sought a new object of attack. With increased reinforcements, they swept down on the abandoned fort, where for the following hour they took out on the buildings and barricades all of their frustrated wrath. It was as if they had finally grabbed a forbidden fruit that had long been denied them. They left nothing standing which the rebels had constructed. Walls were demolished, camp sites scattered, and fortifications put to the torch. Even the graves of the Bábís were desecrated, and in some instances bodies exhumed and burned. Only the shrine of Shaykh Ṭabarsí remained unscathed.

With the dust of their deeds still unsettled, the troops set their eyes on a bigger prize. Regrouping outside the ravaged fortress, they bolstered each other's courage with battle cries. "Let us avenge the deaths of our comrades," a sword-waving trooper cried. "The Bábís are not far away," yelled another. Pointing his saber in the direction of the helpless encampment, he roared at the top of his voice, "*Alláh-u Akbar,*" a signal which sent the excited horsemen racing off.

While this scene unfolded, the three companions had parted from Abdu'llah and journeyed some distance from the camp. Finding a large shade tree, they had sat down to await the return of Quddús. Hasan was still anxious to pursue the earlier conversation. "And even if Quddús knows what he is doing," he said, "what will become of us?"

"God will guide us," Amin shot back without hesitation.

"That he may. But we will still have to make decisions. To this point our Master, Sayyid-i Báb, has not freed himself, and I dare say that without him we are leaderless."

"Quddús has been given that role," Amin said confidently. "After he has returned from his consultation with the prince, he will inform us of his intentions."

Hasan sat back and thought. At Badasht Amin had appeared to be at odds with Quddús, sometimes even hostile. Lately, however, he seemed to agree with whatever he did. Was this because without Qurratu'l-'Ayn to lead him Amin was pulled back under the commander's dominant hand? Or was it the result of combat? Or even perhaps the feeling that now Quddús was someone special? He fished for an answer. "You know there are some who feel that Quddús is the Qá'im."

"That is blasphemy," thundered Amin.

"Argument will not do us any good," 'Ali interrupted. Whatever happens, we must remain unified. When we are removed from under the prince's yoke we will be free to act, and with God's blessings we will make the right decisions."

"But that is what I was asking," continued Hasan, undaunted. "How will those—?"

Hasan's sentence was never finished. As the words left his mouth the men were startled by the yells of their companions. They looked back in the direction of the camp and saw men scurrying here and there in a state of near frenzy. "What's happened?" yelled Hasan. "Is it an attack?"

"I think so," shouted Amin. "We had better move."

When they were only a few yards from their tent, they were met by Abdu'llah. His frantic voice confirmed the worst. "Grab your swords! The government troops are attacking!"

The scene around them was one of chaos and disaster. Everywhere they looked, their comrades were falling to the ground amid uninterrupted volleys of gunfire. The entire camp appeared to be covered by a swarm of gray uniforms. Instinctively, each of the companions knew that there was little hope of repelling the attack. Nevertheless, there was no thought of abandoning their duty, and all three sallied forth to meet the waves of onrushing enemy troops.

The next few minutes were horror. While the rifle fire

took its deadly toll, the soldier's swords rained blows like hailstones. From one side of the encampment to the other, bloodstained steel flashed as the government troops tore at the wounded flesh of their reeling adversaries. To an outside observer, the surrounding tableau would have resembled cornered deer being ripped to pieces by a pack of hungry wolves. Yet, regardless of their hopeless situation, the assailed Bábís fought with the conviction that had become their trademark. Time and again they charged headlong into the relentless assault.

By the time the last wave of enemy horsemen had swept through the encampment, over half of the Bábís had fallen. As the gray-clad warriors regrouped to make their second pass, it was apparent that it would not be long before the massacre was complete. With this knowledge pulsating in their breasts, the exhausted and leaderless men prepared themselves for their last act of defiance. Some were so fatigued they could barely stand, while others who still had energy left scurried to the dead bodies of their fallen comrades to replace lost or broken weapons. In not one instance did the thought of surrender enter their minds; all accepted what they knew must come.

They did not have to wait long. From the center of the bellowing troops, whose snorting horses formed a solid wall of black and brown, a solitary saber was raised aloft. Without further hesitation, the cavalry charged forward, the dust from their bolting steeds spiraling slowly upward into the cloudless sky.

Both Hasan and Amin were among those who had so far managed to escape the government bullets. When the troops began the second charge, they found themselves next to one another on the far right side of the Bábí formation. Ali, however, had been drawn to the center of the battleground, where he and the Bábís around him were again forced to take the brunt of the final onslaught. As in the first strike, both rifle and saber pounded down on them. Only their last reserves of will allowed them to keep their own swords in the air.

Soon the entire force of rebels was engulfed, and every member of the party found himself engaged in individual combat. Many were forced to contend with two men at once. Were it not for the fact that they were fighting at such close quarters, most would have been easy prey for their mounted enemy. But the jostling of horses and lack of turning space actually gave them some degree of protection. Such was the case with Hasan, who found himself virtually pinned between two animals. Ironically, the position allowed him a vantage point to one of his assailant's unprotected ribs, while at the same time shielding him from the second attacker. With this opportunity before him, he thrust his sword forward. Following a line directed just below the sternum, the cold steel blade penetrated the man's flesh and entered his flaccid stomach. To the accompaniment of a nerve-shattering scream, Hasan pushed on his sword. Then, without waiting to see the result of his blow, he withdrew the blade and turned to face his second foe.

The image that confronted him as he twirled around was that of a wild-eyed horseman, his sword raised and ready to strike. Although there was no more than a split second between the moment he saw the soldier and the downward movement of his sword, Hasan's mind vividly recorded his enemy's face. Covered with stubble soaked in perspiration and dust, and dominated by two huge eyes whose deep black pupils were surrounded by thin streaks of red, the face was one he had seen many times as a child in the meat markets of Shiraz. Now it was he, and not the young calf, who was the object of those fiery eyes. Quickly shifting from the past to the present, he raised his own sword above his head, an act which caused the falling steel blade to glance sideward and miss its mark. Then, with lightning speed, he hurled his blade upward, catching the now unbalanced horseman on the side of the neck. A spray of purple covered both beast and rider. Dropping his weapon, the man reached for his gaping wound. His gesture was useless. With the blood oozing through his fingers, the soldier toppled to the ground, while his horse bolted wildly from the field of battle.

Hasan finished the fallen trooper off with a slash to the side of his head and then wheeled around in time to see Ali deliver a devastating blow to one of the unit's officers. Not only did the man lose half of his arm, he was knocked completely off his careening horse. Thumping to the ground several yards away, the wounded officer lay motionless as the young Bábí prepared to complete his work. But seeing their leader's plight, a number of his men dismounted, abandoned their animals, and rushed to his aid.

With reflex-like quickness Hasan summed up the situation and cried out to his brother, "Amin, follow me!" Dashing toward the riderless horses, he grabbed one of them by the reins and threw himself on its back. Close behind him, Amin did likewise. Quickly adjusting to the saddles, they both rode off into the center of the fray.

Fighting their way forward, the brothers again spotted Ali, who was now assailed on all sides by flashing metal. Pointing to their beseiged comrade, Hasan gave a sharp kick to the strange animal beneath him, and without looking back, pounced on one of the attackers. He was about to lean down to help Ali up when a slashing blade caught his friend on the top of his turban. The blow split the top of his head, causing Ali to throw up his arms before falling to the ground in a blood-splattered heap.

Hasan looked up and saw that the assailant was the same lieutenant who had delivered the Qur'an to the fort. Almost immediately he heard a cry. Throwing his body around, he saw Amin slumped in his saddle, his right arm tightly grasping his left. From the wound ran a deep red rivulet, whose pulsating flow told Hasan that the blade had penetrated an artery. Abandoning thoughts of chasing the lieutenant, he redirected his horse to help his wounded brother. In seconds he was at Amin's side. Putting an arm around him, he pulled the grimacing youth onto his own animal. "Hold on," he yelled, and headed toward a small gap which had opened in front of him.

As it turned out, the gap was a break in the enemy lines. Seizing on the opportunity, Hasan spurred the horse forward. Before any of the enemy had noticed, the brothers were in full flight.

When he was clear from the melee, Hasan brought the steed to a halt, and turned him around. He looked back from where they had come. One glance told him that the slaughter was complete. The last struggling remnants of a once proud force were now entirely surrounded.

"Those cowards," whispered Hasan. "I will find that lieutenant one day." Then, tightening his free arm around Amin, he rode off to the safety of the nearby forest.

WHEN THEY RETURNED the next morning to the scene of the battle, the brothers were confronted with a gruesome sight. The camp itself had been pillaged, the corpses of their fallen comrades mutilated. Hacked and disembowled bodies were strewn over a large area. In several instances the remains had been heaped together and burned. As for survivors, none were to be found anywhere.

As Hasan staggered over the battlefield, numb but with a rising nausea, he came across the decapitated body of Ali. Hasan recognized his friend's distinctive gray woolen robe, now stained a color between rusty-brown and reddish-black, harboring at least a dozen flies and several hundred hunger-crazed ants. Hasan turned away and vomited.

As they continued their search, they found old Abdu'llah. In a similar fashion, during the next hour they were able to identify another ten of their close friends, some by facial features, others by some detail of their apparel.

"How could we have been so stupid?" said Hasan, gazing at the sickening landscape.

"Quddús did the right thing," retorted Amin, sliding his free hand under his bandaged arm to give it more support. "We could not disrespect their pledge on the Qur'an . . . Death is death, whether by sword or starvation."

"But there is no dignity in having one's body disfigured."

"Do you think it would have been any different if they had waited for us to die? Wild dogs are wild dogs. The only thing I regret is that you didn't allow me to remain here and die with them."

"And what good would that have done?"

"It is a matter of dignity."

Hasan did not answer. His only concern now was that they should not be seen. The dust rising from the government camp indicated that the troops were preparing to depart, but there was no guarantee that a trailing surveillance party was not nearby. There was only time to water their horse and refresh their own dry throats. There would be days to discuss the wisdom of his move. Hasan made his way to the well and readied himself for their return to the forest.

Chapter 12

THE ROAD LEADING to the mosque of the Sa'ídu'l-'Ulamá was narrow and dusty. The powdery haze which the two dozen horsemen kicked up was signal enough to cause a stirring among the people who inhabited the small mud-plaster houses dotting its edges. As the riders passed the first of these dwellings, a number of the local residents came to their doorways to get a better view. The sight that first met their eyes was not an unusual one. As on many occasions in the past, they watched as government troops passed through their town. However, this time on closer inspection they noticed an irregularity. One of the men among the riders was not wearing a uniform. Moreover, although his hands were free to guide the reins, his arms were tightly bound to the sides of his body by several lashings of rope.

Within each household speculation began to rise as to the identity of the prisoner. Some thought he was a thief being brought to justice, and they cringed at the thought of him losing his hand. Others guessed that he was an army defector. Some, who were aware of the events that had taken place at the shrine of Shaykh Ṭabarsí, knew that he must be one of the heretics known as Bábís.

When the troop reached its destination, the captain and two junior officers dismounted and helped the man down from his horse. Handling him roughly, they did not bother to untie his arms, but led him directly to the interior of the large house of worship. Weak from lack of food and water, Quddús followed his captors. As a sign of disgrace, he was without his headdress: the green turban had been confiscated by the mullás of Bárfurúsh at the mock hearing he was given in front of Prince Mihdí. It was then that the prince had washed his hands of the whole affair and handed the rebel leader over to the mullás.

Quddús was taken to a small room where he was bound to a wooden beam. "There," said the captain, jerking the rope tighter with relish. "May you get what you deserve." Motioning to his fellow officers, he began to leave the chamber. "Captain," said Quddús in a scratchy voice, "may I have some water?"

The officer stopped. "The Sa'ídu'l-'Ulamá will decide what you can and cannot have. My orders were to bring you here—no more, no less." With those words, the captain left.

His body aching from fatigue, Quddús slumped forward. Only the ropes that bound him to the timber post kept him aright. In a semiconscious state, his mind began to wander, taking him to the sacred city of Mecca. He was with the Báb; they were completing the circumambulation of the most holy shrine. Unexpectedly, his Master left his side. Standing against the structure of the Kaaba, the Báb took hold of the ring on its door and proclaimed three times in a loud and clear voice. "I am that Qá'im whose advent you await."

This image dissolved into another scene from the past. Again they were in Mecca, but this time the site was the roof of the pilgrimage house where the two travelers had lodged. His Master was again speaking. "O Quddús," He said, "you who have believed in me. I take you at this moment as my witness. I declare that the hostility of every mullá of the land will not stop this Cause. Neither words nor swords nor bullets will keep it from its purpose."

Suddenly, with a shock, Quddús was back in Bárfurúsh,

water dripping from his nose and chin. In front of him stood the Sa'ídu'l-'Ulamá, a huge grin covering his face. "I was told that you were thirsty," he snickered. "Unfortunately, you were asleep when I offered you a drink, and, alas, it has spilled on the floor."

Quddús used nearly all of his strength to raise his head. He squinted at the man in front of him. Although his vision was partially blurred, he could still make out the main features of the mullá's thin, craggy face. Bordered on one side by his black turban, and on the other by a profusion of grey hairs, the Sa'ídu'l-'Ulamá's contorted countenance gave him a frightful, almost sinister look which the captive thought more appropriate for a demon than a man of God.

"Want more?" the mullá asked. Again dousing Quddus, he sent the brass goblet hurtling to the floor. With the sound of the crashing metal still vibrating through the room, the mullá snapped out another question. "You know what the penalty for murder is don't you?"

No longer able to keep his head up, Quddús allowed it to hang freely, leaving the question unanswered.

"Didn't you hear me?" shouted the Sa'ídu'l-'Ulamá.

Again Quddús gave no reply.

As anger welled up within him, the mullá reached forward and grabbed the Bábí by the hair. Pushing Quddús's head backward, he forced the prisoner to look at him. "Don't you even have the dignity to admit your crimes? You are no better than a common criminal. Yet you had the audacity to wear a green turban. You will learn that such insolence will not be tolerated."

With great difficulty, Quddús strained his already weakened voice to give the mullá his answer. "I have committed no crime."

"The murder of a mullá is no crime?" yelled the Sa'ídu'l-'Ulamá. "Do you deny that the group under your command was responsible for the deaths of a number of our townspeople including a mullá?"

Quddús did not tell the enraged divine that he was not present at the episode to which he was referring. Instead, he used his strength to defend the honor of his men. "They were attacked by a mob," he groaned. "They were defending themselves."

"Now you stoop to add lying to your inventory of sins," scoffed the Sa'ídu'l-'Ulamá. "As you know, those people were killed in cold blood. They were defenseless citizens."

The mullá forced Quddús's head back even further. "You contemptuous dog," he spit out. "You will get your justice." Violently yanking the man's beard, he loudly summoned one of his aides.

When the small, turbanless boy arrived, the Sa'ídu'l-'Ulamá instructed him to fetch the cane. The lad obediently left for the far end of the building. A few moments later, he returned with the instrument, then withdrew, politely bowing.

The weapon was a three-foot-long willow branch, its thick end wrapped in several layers of tightly bound cloth. Tapering down to a fine flexible rod, it was an innocent-looking but highly effective instrument of pain. In the hands of the Sa'ídu'l-'Ulamá, it was as dreaded as a sharpened sword.

While the boy carried out his errand, the Sa'ídu'l-'Ulamá called the captain and his junior officers and instructed them to move Quddús to a nearby room where he was to be tied face down to a wooden bench. By the time the cane was in the mullá's hand, this task had been accomplished. Thus, when the Sa'ídu'l-'Ulamá entered the room, his victim lay sprawled before him—ready to receive the fury of his wrath.

"Do you have any further request, my lord?" asked the captain, hoping that he might be allowed to leave.

"Remove his boots," ordered the Sa'ídu'l-'Ulamá.

The most junior of the officers approached the prostrate Quddús. One boot at a time, he pulled the dusty footwear from the prisoner's feet.

"Go now," said the Sa'ídu'l-'Ulamá.

"Yes, sir," the captain replied.

They bowed politely and were about to leave, when the divine again stopped them. "Wait," he cried. "Perhaps you should observe how we punish a heretic?"

The officers knew that the Sa'ídu'l-'Ulamá's comment was not a suggestion. They halted abruptly and turned to face the black-cloaked mullá, who was swishing the willow branch back and forth through the air, filling the room with the shrill sounds of its high-pitched whistle.

After several more trials he was ready to test his skill on living flesh. Lightly he rubbed the end of the cane against Quddús's bare soles. "This is for having the audacity to wear a green turban," he roared. Waving the cane above his head, he brought it forcefully against its tender target.

A streak of pain shot through Quddús's leg. Instinctively, he sought to pull his feet free, but this only caused the rope to cut into his exposed ankles. Again the cane hit its target; and again Quddús's body convulsed. The third blow came quicker and with greater force. It was followed almost immediately by a fourth, fifth, and sixth stroke. The Sa'ídu'l-'Ulamá was working himself into a frenzy as the air filled with the whistle of the cane and the snap of its strike.

Despite the extreme pain, Quddús made no sound—a reaction which infuriated his tormentor even more. "Why doesn't your Qá'im rescue you?" screamed the mullá, striking him again and again.

Breathing heavily, his face covered with perspiration, the divine paused. Dropping the rod to his side, he glanced at the captain. "Our rebel doesn't seem so rebellious now."

The captain nodded in agreement.

"You know," continued the Sa'ídu'l-'Ulamá, walking toward the end of the table that supported Quddús's head, "there is no chance that beloved leader of yours will ever be set loose again . . . But, if you were willing to publicly recant your belief in him, I would do all that is in my power to see that you might go free."

In spite of the pain that his body and mind were experiencing, on hearing these words Quddús found a reservoir of energy on which to draw. Painfully, he lifted his head from the table. "I would rather roast in hell!"

In an outburst of fury, the Sa'ídu'l-'Ulamá raised the willow and sent it whistling down to the back of Quddús's neck, causing the prisoner's raised head to slam against the table beneath him. "You will get your wish soon enough," the mullá whispered and once more rained blows on the defiant Bábí.

THE NEXT MORNING, word spread throughout the city that there would be a public flogging that afternoon. By the time the sun was at its zenith, a number of men, first in small clusters, and then in large groups, began to gather in the sprawling square that fronted the mosque. At three o'clock, with the words of the *adhan* echoing in the streets, the Sa'íd'ul-'Ulamá stepped into the courtyard to lead the afternoon prayer. This duty was usually reserved for a younger man, but today the mullá had decided, for reasons known only to him, that he would take charge.

Standing in front of the congregation, his black robe fluttering in the breeze, he began the ritual maneuvers. Raising his hands to his ears, he boomed forth in his loudest voice, "God is Most Great. *Alláh-u Akbar.*" Behind him, men in straight lines followed his example. Next he performed, one after another, the appropriate positions of prayer: standing, bowing, prostrating, sitting—separating each one with the correct phrases and verses. Four times he repeated the process, his every move and utterance closely mimicked by the faithful. Spouting forth another declaration of faith, he brought the session to its conclusion.

As the congregation rose to its feet, the Sa'ídu'l-'Ulamá turned to address its members. "Followers of the Apostle of God," he began. "When our Prophet—peace be upon him—gave us the gift of our religion, he warned us that there would arise those agents of evil who would try to destroy it. Recent events throughout our land have shown that his prediction has come to pass. There are circulating among us, feigning to be men of God, the agents of Satan himself. However, due to the efforts of the ulama, and with the aid of the imperial throne, the leader of this group has been apprehended and locked away in the mountains far to the north. Nevertheless, many of his followers are still spreading his soul-destroying doctrines.

"In the last few months," he continued, "a band of his disciples infested our province, killing our people and causing havoc in our cities. Fortunately, a large body of these rebels has been put to the sword by the imperial army on the plains near the shrine of Shaykh Ṭabarsí, whose hallowed grounds they had the audacity to inhabit. The commander of this group has been brought here to Bárfurúsh. As an example of the fruits of heresy, he will receive today the prescribed punishment of flogging, with the opportunity to recant publicly. Should he refuse to admit his errors, he will be dealt with in the manner befitting anyone who seeks to ruin the religion of the Prophet of God.''

When his speech was finished, the Sa'ídu'l-'Ulamá turned in the direction of the mosque and slowly raised his hand into the air. There appeared in the doorway the figure of Quddús, a guard at each side.

''There he is,'' shouted the mullá. And on cue the crowd began to howl and jeer.

Now in the sunlight, the three men made their way toward the square. To those who were watching closely, it soon became evident that the prisoner was having difficulty walking. He leaned on his escorts, allowing them to carry him along without moving his legs. It was also apparent that this maneuver was annoying the guards, who kept trying to make the man support his own weight by shoving him upright after every few steps. This effort, however, only succeeded in making him stumble and, on several occasions, nearly fall. Consequently, the men in gray were forced to accept that they would have to guide him toward their destination. In this way, stopping and starting, the trio slowly traversed the fifty yards that separated the annex from the wall surrounding the courtyard.

Several long minutes later they arrived. Lifting Quddús's arms aloft, the soldiers bound his hands to the two iron rings that protruded from the center of the clay barrier. Stripping him of his shirt, they turned and saluted the smirking mullá. "Wait here," he told them. After another hurried salute, the guards backed unobtrusively into the front row of the crowd.

The next few minutes saw the Sa'ídu'l-'Ulamá dispense forty lashes. Today it was Quddús's back which took the stinging pain that only the day before this feet had borne. But whereas on the prior occasion he had felt at times that he might falter in his resolve, now each application of the lash gave him more strength. Although the pain was great, he knew that he could not be broken.

When the last snap of the cane had sounded, the Sa'ídu'l-'Ulamá gestured to the guards to free Quddús's hands from their iron shackles. His back torn and bleeding, the rebel leader was taken down from the wall and paraded before his cursing audience. All he could do was hang precariously to the shoulders of his escorts.

Callously, the Sa'ídu'l-'Ulamá approached the limp, almost lifeless body of Quddús. "O evil one," he shouted. "Have you seen the error of your ways? Do you renounce Sayyid 'Alí-Muḥammad and his teachings?"

The crowd became quiet. But, their suspense was not long lived. Awkwardly straightening himself, Quddús answered. "Forgive, O my God, the trespasses of this people. Deal with them in thy mercy, for they know not what I have already discovered and cherish."

Filled with uncontrollable rage, the Sa'ídu'l-'Ulamá grasped the small ax concealed beneath his black robe and pulled it out. His hands trembling, he raised the weapon to eye level and thrust it forward, delivering a crushing blow to the side of Quddús's head. As soon as the metal blade made contact with his skin, the prisoner fell to his knees, blood spurting from the wound in well-defined gushes. With the Bábí now beneath him, the mullá swung again, striking the top of Quddús's skull and causing him to topple over on his side.

Then it was the crowd's turn. Retreating, the Sa'ídu'l-'Ulamá left the crumpled man to receive their wrath. Using knives, rocks, or any instrument they could get their hands on, the frenzied mob tore at Quddús like hungry lions before a kill, and with the same grisly results. What was once a human body soon became a pile of ribboned flesh, dismembered and disfigured. Only the flames of the fire that the Sa'ídu'l-'Ulamá ordered built would remove the mutilated sight from the eyes of passers-by. But even as those embers were burning themselves out, the fuel for a still greater conflagration was being gathered in Tabriz.

Chapter 13

THE LAST SHADOWS OF DAY were falling as Hasan and Amin passed under the southernmost gateway leading into Tabriz. The brothers had planned their arrival to coincide with the coming of evening, for although they had not set foot in the city since their departure east, they were still fearful that they might be recognized. And they hoped the darkness would conceal their destination: the home of one of the Báb's most loyal and faithful followers.

It had been over a year since they had left the catastrophic scene on the plain beyond Fort Ṭabarsí. For some time they had kept to themselves, living almost a hermit's existence in the mountains of Mazandaran. Even when they had finally decided to return to the cities, they had done so guardedly, making sure that they spent no more than a month in any one place and usually remaining in hiding at the homes of friends.

Their fears were not unfounded. During the last twelve months, followers of the Báb had been attacked and persecuted throughout the country. The upheaval in Mazandaran had set off a chain of hatred and violence. Only four months before, seven of their comrades had been publicly executed in the capital. Even now, as they made their entry into Tabriz, the events of Ṭabarsí were being repeated in Zanján and Nayríz.

Winding their way through the streets and alleyways of the southern section of the city, the men finally stopped their horses in front of a small, plaster-walled building. Here they dismounted. They secured their animals to the iron gate bordering the rose-encircled dwelling and hurried toward its threshold. Amin applied three sharp raps to the door, and moments later the large wooden portal swung open. For several seconds the face confronting them stared in disbelief. Finally, Mírzá Reza expressed his unhidden sentiments. "Amin!" he gasped. "We thought that you were dead."

Amin stepped forward to accept Mírzá Reza's embrace. "Tell me," he said urgently, "is it true they are going to execute our Beloved?"

"Yes," Reza replied as he let go of Amin. "But come in. It is not safe to discuss such things in the open."

The two brothers followed their host through the doorway and into the waiting area. "This is my brother Hasan," said Amin. "He joined us at Badasht."

"It is indeed a pleasure to meet you Hasan," said Mírzá Reza. "You are both welcome here at any time. My house is yours. Now, please, there are several friends I want you to meet." He led them through the folds of a velvet partition.

The room they entered was small, but well furnished. Seated on two exquisite silk-covered divans were four men, all adorned in beige robes and wearing a variety of dark turbans. In front of them, supporting glasses of tea, were two finely carved wooden tables, while on the wall behind them hung a large carpet whose colorful geometric patterns were sure to mesmerize any onlooker. Similar rugs covered the floor, giving the three smaller tables resting on them a cushioned base. Upon all the tables sat numerous brass ornaments, varying in shape from a peacock to a mounted soldier. These were accompanied by several small paintings, whose dainty miniature subjects more than complimented their bolder brass companions.

As soon as the seated men saw the newly arrived guests, they stood up. Mírzá Reza hurriedly pulled in two pillows from a nearby pile. "Make yourselves comfortable," he said, gesturing toward the cushions. "You know everyone here, Amin. I will see to it that your horses are taken around back."

While their host left to attend to his task, Amin introduced Hasan to the four men. The most senior of the group was Sayyid Manshadi, a local inhabitant who had been with the Báb since the beginning of his mission. To his immediate left sat Hasan-i Kirmani, a carpenter from the south who had been converted by Quddús during the latter's first missionary journey. On the second divan sat two younger men, Mírzá Rahim and Najaf-'Alí, both from Tehran. Amin had met all of them in the capital before leaving for Badasht.

By the time the formal introductions and greetings were finished, Mírzá Reza was back among them. Seating himself next to Kirmani, the brown-turbaned gentleman looked at Amin. "So you escaped from Ṭabarsí?" he said. "We heard that everyone at the fort was killed."

It was Hasan who answered their host's question. "We were tricked into coming out of the fort. They swore on the Qur'an that they would allow us to leave in peace. Then they ambushed us at our temporary camp site."

"How many lost their lives?"

"In all, over three hundred and fifty," replied Amin ". . . But these men are gone; they cannot be brought back. Should we not be concerning ourselves with the plight of our Lord?"

"We were just discussing the situation," Reza explained. "It has come as a shock to all of us."

"Then his execution is a certainty?" asked Hasan.

"Apparently," interjected Sayyid Manshadi. "Tomorrow there is to be a hearing which, from the information we have, will only be a formality."

"But why the sudden decision?" Amin cried. "He couldn't have committed any crime in that mountain prison."

"For one thing," said Kirmani, breaking in, "the death of the shah. While he was alive, our Beloved was safe, for Muḥammad S͟háh was much opposed to executions on religious grounds. Our new king, Náṣiri'd-Dín, however, shares no such conviction. Moreover, his new minister, Mírzá Taqí K͟hán, seems determined to stamp out the Cause. He will not be satisfied until the Báb is dead."

"Still, they will have to use some excuse," said Amin. "Some charge will have to be laid."

"A charge will be found," said Sayyid Manshadi. "The disturbances throughout the country have become a source of embarrassment to the Grand Vizier, and he plans to eliminate the problem at its source."

"The official charge will most likely be the dissemination of heretical literature," added Najaf-'Alí. "Not long ago I met our Beloved's courier, Ali Guzal, who had been with him in C͟híríq. He reported that after Ṭabarsí and the execution of Quddús, Sayyid-i Báb sent many Tablets to various parts of the country. It now appears that some of these writings have fallen into the hands of the mullás. This will give Mírzá Taqí K͟hán all the excuse he needs."

"I have heard similar reports," said Reza. "And one of these Tablets apparently makes mention of One who will succeed the Báb when he is gone."

Just as Reza had finished speaking, the servant entered the room with glasses of tea for the new guests. The servant offered them the tea then quickly retired behind the partition, leaving the men to continue their discussion.

"Tell us more about this Tablet," said Hasan as he lowered the glass from his lips.

"I think it is more important to discuss what we can do to help our Lord," countered Amin sharply. "There does not seem to be a great deal of concern here about what we can do."

Mírzá Reza leaned forward, and Hasan could tell from the look on his face that he had suddenly become extremely serious. "It is not that we haven't given it thought," he said. "But the problem is a difficult one. There seems only one hope: that they don't give him the death sentence. If they do, there is virtually nothing that can be done. He is heavily guarded, and we have neither the manpower nor the firepower to free him. What is more, any attempt to rescue him would only endanger his life."

Amin was quick to reply. "If he is to be executed, I don't see why we should be worried about endangering his life. It may be an outside chance, but it is a risk we must take."

"It is not just a matter of endangering our Master's life," said Sayyid Manshadi, emphasizing his statement with a tightening of his hands. "Any attempt to rescue the Báb would put the lives of all his followers and their families in jeopardy. We have seen how vicious the mullás can be, and with Taqí Khán behind them there is no limit to the suffering they can cause."

"Then are we to sit here and do nothing?" pleaded Amin.

"For the moment, perhaps the best thing to do is wait until after the hearing," said Reza. "We have an informer inside the court who can relay the decision to us as soon as it is handed down. When we know the verdict, we can decide a course of action."

A buzz of approval indicated that the friends were in

agreement with their host's proposal. Although Amin felt uneasy about the lack of resolution, he remained silent.

"Then we will meet tomorrow." Reza suddenly rose to his feet and faced Sayyid Manshadi. "As soon as you know the verdict, inform the others and come here immediately. Amin and Hasan will spend the night with me, so we will have no trouble assembling quickly."

"Certainly, my honorable friend." Sayyid Manshadi made a reverent gesture. "When I receive word I will contact the others."

"Very good," replied Reza. "And may God be with you."

The group exchanged embraces and dispersed. Sayyid Manshadi and his three companions set off into the night, and Mírzá Reza with his two guests moved to the back of the house to prepare themselves for a much-desired sleep.

A VIGOROUS KNOCK on the door startled the three sleeping men. Springing up from the divan, Reza did not wait for his servant, but hurried to the source of the sound and threw open the wooden door. Before him stood Sayyid Manshadi, his brow covered with sweat and his chest heaving. "Quickly," he whispered hoarsely. "There has been no hearing, and they are taking him at this very moment to the execution ground!"

"What?" stammered Reza, almost unable to believe what he was hearing. "What do you mean there was no hearing?"

"He was taken to Mámáqání's mosque, but the mullá said that since he had not surrendered any of his doctrines, the death warrant would be signed at once. The only thing that was necessary was identification."

"Isn't there any sense of justice left?" cried Amin, now standing behind Reza.

"There is no time to discuss the matter," Sayyid Manshadi said urgently. "We must get to the citadel square immediately."

"You are right," said Reza. "Words will not change anything." Hastily summoning his servant, he ordered him to prepare the horses.

"I will go now," said the panting messenger. "Meet me at the open end of the square."

"Yes, you go," agreed Reza. "We will not be far behind."

Not long after, when the three men arrived at the citadel square, a large crowd was already present. Located on the western side of Tabriz's main fortress, the parade ground was defined by its rectangular gravel surface which stretched lengthwise from the back of the citadel wall to a small sentry post some seventy-five yards away. Along each side ran barracks whose rooftops would provide the primary viewing area for the excited spectators. Several hundred yards from the sentry post was another set of barracks in whose rooms was housed the man they had come to see.

The anxious Bábís tied their horses behind a nearby row of shops, concealed their weapons beneath their clothing, and moved hastily toward the open end of the square. Here they found Sayyid Manshadi consulting with a number of men, two of whom included Mírzá Rahim and Najaf-'Alí. Careful not to be overheard, Mírzá Reza touched his friend's shoulder and whispered into his ear: "Can we do anything?"

Sayyid Manshadi made a gesture of futility. "He is completely surrounded by soldiers." He nodded in the direction of the far barracks. "His fate is sealed."

Mírzá Reza looked toward the building to which Sayyid Manshadi was referring. It was completely surrounded by troops. Only a small section at the far end was not obscured by gray uniforms. "You are right," he said. "Only God can save him now."

"I am going up," announced Amín in a voice that could be heard by all. With Hasan close to his side, he began to move toward the crowded stairway which led to the barracks roof.

"Come, let's join him," suggested Mírzá Reza.

Sayyid Manshadi's abrupt movement toward the stairs provided his answer. The rest of the men in the small circle followed.

While his followers were jostling for a position on the rooftop, the Báb was brought out of his cell and directed toward the barracks door by heavily armed guards. At his side was a young man. As the two stepped into the daylight to begin their journey down the weather-beaten pathway which would take them to their deaths, they were greeted by a chorus of bawling derision. As with all public executions, the devout had assembled to see justice done.

As the two men were being led toward the square, a soldier from the regiment carrying out the execution was busy hammering a large iron spike into the middle of the citadel wall. By the time he had finished, the prisoners and their guard escort had reached the far end of the quadrangle and were beginning the last leg of their march across the parade ground. Moving slowly in the direction of the iron rod, they continued to receive the curses of the boisterous spectators. As they passed beneath the western barracks, the verbal insults turned into even more threatening forms of hostility. Sheets of saliva showered down, and several rocks thudded to the ground beside them. Only the fact that the guards themselves began to feel threatened caused their course to be altered, and so for the last thirty yards the small party stayed well clear of the barracks and the missiles of spittle and stone.

Looking down, the Báb's disciples watched helplessly as their leader was mocked and ridiculed. Hasan's anger boiled within him. Amin was so overcome with grief that he could not watch the procession; instead he cast his eyes down at the stone-covered roof beneath him. Even the normally calm Reza could barely control his emotions; at one point he nearly threw himself on a rock-throwing spectator. Only the quick reactions of Sayyid Manshadi, who saw what he was about to do and restrained his arms, prevented an incident.

Regaining his composure, Reza wondered about the identity of the man accompanying the Báb. His question was inadvertently answered by a nearby onlooker who was loudly explaining the situation to a small group of men surrounding him. "The one with him is a follower," he said. "You can see by his age that he is only a boy. The evil one does not care in the slightest whom he corrupts."

Reza looked in the direction of Sayyid Manshadi, his eyes asking for more information. Recognizing his request, the disciple leaned on his friend and responded in a low voice. "His name is Mírzá Muḥammad-'Alí; you have met him. Apparently, as our Lord was being taken to the barracks he threw himself at His feet and pleaded not to be sent away. The mullás have seen to it that his wish has been granted."

By now the prisoners had arrived at the citadel wall. Behind them, the Fourth Armenian Regiment was rapidly moving toward the firing area. Rifles on shoulders and marching three abreast, the soldiers' distinctive blue coats with red trim instantly identified them to the noisy crowd. At their head paced the regiment commander, Sám Khán.

While the firing squad slowly moved into position, the Báb's hands were lashed to the iron rod and his body suspended against the citadel wall. The disciple was also bound to the bar, but in a manner that made him hang directly in front of his Master, leaving the sayyid's breast as the sole resting place for his turbanless head.

When they were finally affixed to one another, the escorts moved behind the riflemen, who had already loaded their weapons and formed themselves into three long lines. The first row was stretched out on their stomachs; the second knelt; and the third remained on their feet. Those on their stomachs had their rifles beside them, while the men on their knees and feet kept their weapons upright. Meanwhile, Sám Khán paraded nervously up and down in front of them, making sure that all was ready.

Finally, the commander took up his position at one side of his troops. On the rooftop, Hasan and Amin watched in almost dreamlike silence as the officer raised his arm into the air. To both brothers there was an air of unreality about the setting in which they found themselves. Hasan wanted to act, yet some paralyzing inner force prevented him from doing anything but watch the unfolding drama below. The faithful Amin could not quite fathom the fact that his beloved Master was about to be shot.

Abruptly Sám Khán's arm fell. With this signal, each row of blue-coated soldiers opened fire, the men on their stomachs shooting first, followed in quick succession by the rows of troops behind them.

As the shots rang out, a series of rocketing echoes, accompanied by a dense cloud of smoke, filled the parade ground. So thick was the smoky haze that for several

132

minutes the onlookers could see nothing. When the smoke finally began to dissipate, the masses had to strain to see the results. . . . What they saw astonished them: standing on the ground in front of the citadel wall, looking greatly bewildered, was Mírzá Muḥammad-‘Alí. The rope which had bound him to the iron rod still dangled from his wrists. As for his Master, he was nowhere to be seen.

Sounds of amazement began to purl across the parade ground as men on rooftops turned to one another with looks of disbelief. "He is gone!" some exclaimed. "It is a miracle." Amid this tumult the disciples stood spellbound, unable to untangle the emotions of despair and newfound hope.

The companions watched as from his position atop the most easterly of the barracks, the Chief Lictor rushed into the pandemonium below, his amber robe flying in all directions. He screamed at the stunned troops: "Find him! Search every barracks and building. We can't let him get away." Immediately, groups of soldiers responded, some scurrying for the barracks, others for the distant guard-house.

"Send some men to calm the crowd," shouted the lictor in afterthought to the mystified Sám Khán. "Have them tell the people that everything is under control . . . they can inform them that some of the heretic's followers have tried to free him, but they have been caught and are being questioned."

The commander automatically obeyed his superior's command and began shouting out orders, while the lictor himself joined the frantic search.

In the confusion, both the lictor and Sám Khán had forgotten about Mírzá Muḥammad-‘Alí. The boy remained standing at the base of the wall, his hands free and his cloak unsoiled. He was still in a state of shock, not knowing exactly what to do. When the soldiers had raised their rifles to firing position, he had closed his eyes and begun to whisper in prayer. Prepared to die, the next thing he experienced was a falling sensation which he mistook for death's embrace. Hitting the ground with a sudden thud, he had opened his eyes to see a massive cloud in front of him, an image which his disoriented mind translated as the gates of paradise. It was only after the haze began to clear, and he could identify the scurrying blue coats around him, that he realized he was still alive. But even though he had come to his senses, he was unable to act. He could only stand motionless in the spot where he had landed.

Meanwhile, the hunt went on. One by one, the rooms in both barracks were systematically searched. Small patrols roamed the periphery of the compound looking for any sign that might indicate the Báb's whereabouts. At the same time, the crowd was reassured that everything was under control, and what could have easily become a major disturbance was temporarily calmed by the soldiers' promising words. Still, it was clear that if the Báb were not found, the confusion would soon become a riot.

When the companions heard the guards' explanations, they knew that their stories were false. Nearly every one of them felt instinctively that the miracle for which they had been waiting had taken place. Hasan and Reza wanted to leave and plan for the consequences of such a prodigious event. But Amin persuaded them to stay, for their Master might come out of concealment of any moment. Indeed, such was his enthusiasm that he began to shout aloud his expectations, hoping, as he did, that those around him might see the light and rise to the occasion. "It is a miracle," he cried. "The Qá'im has produced a miracle!"

It was the lictor who finally found the young sayyid. Having searched the far end of the northern barracks without success, he was inexplicably drawn to the small room which had harbored the prisoner during his short stay at the citadel. The door was wide open. Inside the Báb sat conversing with his amanuensis. The startled official knew his duty, but could only gape at the picture before him: the escaped prisoner calmly pouring forth a torrent of words to the furiously writing secretary. Both men were so intensely involved with their tasks that they gave no indication of being aware of the lictor's presence. In fact, it appeared to the man that they were oblivious of everything.

After several minutes, the Báb terminated the chant-like dictation. When the amanuensis placed the pen to his side, he looked at the lictor. "No one on the face of the earth can stop what God hath willed," he said to the benumbed official. "What He commandeth must come to pass."

The lictor knew what the young sayyid was referring to. Earlier that morning, when he had come to take the prisoner to the mujtahids, he had interrupted his conversation with the amanuensis. Now the words which the Báb had directed to him at that time came back as if they were once again being spoken. "Not until I have said to him all those things that I wish to say can any earthly power silence me. Though all the world be armed against me, yet shall they be powerless to deter me from fulfilling to the last word, my intention."

"I have now finished my conversation," declared the Báb, interrupting the lictor's thoughts. "If it is your wish, you may now proceed to fulfill your duty."

A chill of terror ran through the lictor's body. Unable to look his captive in the face, he turned sharply on his heels and ran out of the room, his boots clattering loudly down the narrow corridor of the gloomy barracks. Moments later he was out of the building and in the sunlight, where he encountered the commander of the Nasiri Regiment coming toward him. Like the fleeing lictor, Sám Khán had refused to have anything more to do with the situation and had withdrawn his Armenian Regiment from the parade ground, leaving the Nasiri commander the task of executing his assignment. The officer was on his way to inform the lictor of the change, when he was unexpectedly confronted with the sight of the official dashing from the doorway. He tried to explain, but the lictor brushed past the commander without slowing down or acknowledging him.

The surprised officer shouted at the lictor to stop, but the man ignored him. Realizing that the official was not going to return, he entered the doorway and ran down the corridor. As he approached the cell at the end of the hallway, terror seized his whole being. He entered and found himself looking into the eyes of the Báb. The sayyid was now alone in the room. He made no attempt at resistance but freely offered himself up to the Nasiri commander.

Still confused and fearful, the officer relied on his military instinct. In a booming voice he yelled for assistance. Almost before he had finished, two gray-uniformed soldiers were at his side. "Return him to the wall," he shouted. The larger of the two men responded with a quick salute, and grabbed the placid figure before him. The Báb was pushed out of the cell and down the corridor toward the sunlit doorway.

Over twenty minutes had passed since the crowd had become aware that the Báb was missing. Despite the continual reassurances of the soldiers that he was securely in custody, with each passing minute the spectators grew increasingly restless. Rumors spread that the sayyid had been miraculously delivered from the hands of death, and some of the men around Amin were beginning to voice speculations that perhaps he was the Qá'im after all. But with his sudden reappearance in custody at the far end of the parade ground, the mood abruptly changed once again. Men who had minutes before considered the possibility of the Báb's divinity, returned to railing against him. With all fears now relieved, the vehemence of the throng's attack increased. And as the prisoner crossed the square for the second time, the volume emanating from the rooftops more than matched the pitch that had accompanied his first journey.

As the Báb again approached the citadel wall, the hearts of his followers sank. Their visions of his return with power and glory were dashed. They could only watch mutely as the Qá'im whom they had expected to dispel his adversaries was once more bound with his disciple to the iron bar. Only Amin kept his faith. While the others bowed their heads in silent resignation, his lips quivered with his own private prediction: "Our Lord will be victorious; our Lord will be victorious."

This time no delays were tolerated. The Nasiri Regiment had already filed into the parade ground and taken up its position. As soon as the final knot was tied, they were ready to fire. Unlike the Armenian Regiment, the Nasiris considered it a disgrace to soil their uniforms; consequently, the soldiers in the first row did not assume a prone position but rested on one knee, while both the second and third rows stood erect.

The new commander was anxious to complete his duty. He had just begun to raise his saber when the voice of the Báb boomed forth, echoing across the parade ground and up to the now silent rooftops. "Had you believed in me,

O wayward generation, every one of you would have followed the example of this youth, and willingly sacrificed yourselves in my path. The day will come when you will have recognized me; that day I shall have ceased to be with you."

Again the crowd began to stir, but they were quickly silenced by the commander who yanked his raised sword down. Following his signal, the first row of soldiers opened fire, followed by the second, and the third.

A deafening noise engulfed the citadel, and the parade ground was once more covered with the smoke of discharged rifles. This time, however, the marksmen had hit their target. As the breeze dispersed the chalky cloud, the spectators caught sight of the result. There before them, at the base of the wall, lay the shattered bodies of the Báb and Mírzá Muḥammad-'Alí. What had once been two distinct forms had now become one mass of mangled humanity. Only the Báb's head remained untouched by the fragments of metal, his face still etched with a slight smile.

Their assignment accomplished, the soldiers of the Nasiri Regiment filed out of the parade ground, leaving the remains of their victims behind them. As was customary on such occasions, when the ground was clear of the last soldier, the spectators were given permission to file past the heretics' remains. Some did so with great relish. But most, even some of the most vocal, looked somewhat squeamish as they cast their eyes downward. Others closed their eyes. A few, haunted by the serenity of the sayyid's face, turned and left.

An hour later, the last of the spectators marched past the wall. In another fifteen minutes, the square was completely empty. All that remained were the mutilated corpses and the soldiers whose responsibility it was to gather them up and see to their disposal.

IT WAS NOT UNTIL much later in the day that the bodies of the Báb and his disciple were taken by horse-drawn cart to the easternmost boundary of the city and dumped on the mud-covered edge of the surrounding moat. To make sure that they would be consumed by carnivores and birds of prey, a small party of Nasiri soldiers was stationed to keep watch over them. As heretics, the Báb and his young follower were not to be given a burial, and the mullás wanted to make sure that under no circumstances were their remains retrieved by zealous followers.

While the sun continued to make its westerly descent, and the shadows of late afternoon began to lengthen, dark clouds accumulated on the horizon. What was previously a light and refreshing breeze turned into a strong wind whose gusts swept angrily through the city. The soldiers sitting alongside the moat looked skyward. The clouds advanced on the city, and as they did, the winds grew stronger. Many now found cause to fear for the safety of their property and rushed outside to fasten down, or gather in, those objects which were in danger. Horses neighed wildly in their stables; dogs howled in fear. In the midst of this commotion, swirling dust began to fill the air, adding an eerie quality to the darkness that was slowly engulfing Tabriz.

Suddenly the storm hit with full impact. The heavens opened, pouring sheets of water on the helpless city. Scurrying for cover, the Nasiri guards left their post, abandoning the bodies of the heretics to the fury of the elements. For the next half hour, Tabriz was pounded by wave after wave of lashing rain. Streets flooded, roofs leaked, and shacks toppled. Bewildered families huddled together in the corners of their beseiged homes. Huge flashes of lightning and the accompanying thunderous aftershocks added to the terror. Grown men shivered in fright, and many dropped to their knees to cry out for aid from the Almighty.

As quickly as it had begun, the tempest ended. People slowly came forth from their houses to assess the damage that the storm had caused. In a like manner, the guards emerged from the wooden shack where they had taken refuge and returned to their place of duty. When they arrived, however, the remains of the Báb and his young disciple were gone.

The soldiers looked at each other. "The bodies must have been washed away by the storm," said the leader of the detail. "By now, they are no doubt at the bottom of the moat."

The remaining guards understood that the comment was to be accepted by all. Taking a last look at the flowing stream, they turned to follow their commander back to the cart which would return them to the barracks.

Chapter 14

AMIN WANDERED THROUGH the streets of Tabriz deep in thought. He hardly noticed the busy shops, or the merchants crying out their wares, or the crowds. He could only think of the previous afternoon and the citadel square —the bloodstained wall and the mangled bodies. It was only then, when his eyes beheld the broken figures, that the full impact of the Báb's death had struck him. For although he was aware that the sayyid was being returned to the wall for execution, until that moment he had held onto the hope that his Master's reappearance in the square was only the prologue to an even greater demonstration of divine power. Now that hope was gone, and the young man had to face the reality that his Master was dead.

Amin had left the home of Mírzá Reza early, saying that he was going to the mosque for dawn prayers. Although Hasan wanted to accompany him, he had told his older brother in strong language that he wished to be alone. Fearing for his brother's safety, Hasan tried to have Reza intervene. But the effort was to no avail. Amin refused to discuss the issue. A demand that he return the moment the prayers were completed ended the argument. Yet even under this proviso, Hasan was reluctant to give his consent, only doing so when he realized that his opposition was useless.

The mosque, however, was not Amin's destination. The thought of joining in prayer with those who had killed his beloved leader repulsed him. He would rather consort with swine than share the Holy Word with such hypocrites.

141

Instead, he spent the morning aimlessly rambling through the city's small streets and bazaars, contemplating in an almost dreamlike state the recent events and his own uncertain future.

Turning the corner of a narrow and dusty alleyway, his eyes fell upon a startling scene. In the distance, less than two hundred yards away from the last row of shops, gaped the open end of the citadel square. Somehow, his wanderings had returned him to the spot whose haunting image had obsessed him for the past twenty-four hours. Its sight jolted him into action. As if drawn to the parade ground, he quickened his pace. After a few yards, his walk turned into an open run.

As he drew closer to the barracks, he was hit by an even more staggering vision. There, standing at the base of the wall, was a figure adorned in a green turban, waving his right arm as if he were calling Amin to him. His heart leaping, the young Bábí continued his dash toward the wall. So quickly was he moving, that it was only when he was halfway across the parade ground that the group of guards on morning patrol became aware of his presence. Yelling at him to stop, they set out to make an intercept. Amin's speed, however, was too much for the unprepared soldiers. Before they could seize him, he had reached his destination.

The foot of the wall was still marked with bloodstains from the executions of the previous day. At this exact spot, Amin threw himself to the ground and dug his nails into the reddish clay. "Send me not away from Thee, Master," he cried. "Send me not away from Thee."

Moments later, the guards grabbed the prostrate Amin by the top of his cloak and jerked him to his feet. His face wet with tears, he kept repeating the phrase which had poured forth from his lips as he lay on the ground. It was as if he was in a different world, completely unaware of the men in gray.

"What should we do with him?" said one of the soldiers. "He is obviously out of his mind."

"We had better take him to General Hulagu," answered one of his companions. "He is no doubt one of the heretics."

The two other guards readily agreed. Helping the third swing the still-mumbling Amin around, they guided their prisoner across the parade ground and toward the western barracks.

General Hulagu was engrossed in the pages of his beloved *Shah-Nameh* when the sounds of boots in the hallway outside his door claimed his attention. Placing his glass of tea on the desk and rising to his feet, he commanded his orderly to see what was happening. Automatically, the junior officer departed the room, only to return a few moments later in the company of the three guards and the tightly held Amin. By now the captive had ceased his muttering, and what greeted the general was an emotionless, almost somber face.

"What is the problem here?" General Hulagu stared at Amin. "Who is this man?"

"We found him on the parade ground," answered the tallest of the three guards. "He came running in from the town and prostrated himself in front of the spot where the heretic was executed. As if in a trance, he was calling to his dead leader."

General Hulagu slammed his fist down on the desk in front of him. "Will there be no end to this madness? I am tired of all this nonsense. I have military matters of great urgency to concern myself with. This religious foolishness is waisting my valuable time. Take him to Mámáqání. Let the mullás decide what should be done."

"They will need a written order," whispered the orderly.

"Yes, yes. Where is my pen?" General Hulagu grabbed the pen from his aide and hastily scribbled a message. "Here. Go quickly; Mullá Mámáqání will be at his mosque."

The guard saluted stiffly, clicked his heels together, and turned toward the door. Pulling the passive Amin around with them, the other guards followed. As the relieved general returned to his book, they marched out of his office and began the short trip to the mosque of Tabriz's most eminent mullá.

MULLÁ MÁMÁQÁNÍ PEERED DOWN at the scrawl on the paper which the guard handed to him. Finally deciphering the code, he leaned back in the huge chair that dominated the book-filled room and pensively stroked his full gray beard, all the time eyeing the young man who stood before him. For his part, Amin maintained the blank look he had assumed when the guards had dragged him away from the citadel wall.

"I hope you know that this charge is very serious," growled the mullá brusquely. "Only a man of unsound mind would act in such a manner. Taking this into account, if you are willing to admit to temporary delusion and beg our forgiveness, you will be pardoned."

Amin looked directly into the mullás vacuous eyes. The feelings of fear and anxiety which he had experienced when he was first ushered into the room had vanished. His voice rang out with confidence. "I am not mad," he replied. "Such a charge should rather be brought against you and your cronies who have sentenced to death a man no less holy than the promised Qá'im. He is not a fool who has embraced His faith and is willing to shed his blood in the path of truth."

Mullá Mámáqání deliberately studied Amin's face. What evil spirit, he wondered could cause such insanity? If ever there was need of a proof for the existence of Satan, here it was.

At the same time, Amin's mind was busy at work, pondering how a man who claimed to be a spokesman for the religion of God could be so filled with hate. Was it, he thought, a product of his training, or was he so blinded by his own fears that he could no longer distinguish them from reality?

"Then you will receive your blasphemous desire," yelled the frustrated mullá. "And may your stupidity be an example to those who like yourself are so easily deceived. It is our duty to stamp out this madness before it infects the whole population."

"Do not concern yourself with that," Amin laughed. "This is a madness that can only infect the pure of heart."

Mullá Mámáqání gestured to the guards. "Remove the prisoner," he said in disgust.

Chapter 15

HASAN SPENT A worried and fretful day. When by mid-morning Amin had not returned to the house, the older brother sensed that something was wrong and hurried to the mosque. After hours of fruitlessly searching the building and its environs, he eventually made his way back to Mírzá Reza's home and passed the remainder of the afternoon anxiously discussing the situation with his host. Although they raised every possible reason for not thinking the worst, as the day turned into evening, Hasan's apprehension turned into a feeling of utter helplessness. He was used to having some control over his life; now that circumstances negated his will, he felt disoriented. But worry as he might, he knew that there was nothing he could do but sit and wait.

While Reza shared his guest's emotions, he was able to find a refuge in prayer. Hasan, however, was unable to follow his example. Even at the best of times he found prayer difficult. It had never made sense to him that God's will should be contingent on the requests of men. Perhaps prayer had the value of reconciling one to His will, but Hasan preferred the dynamic of anxiety to the quiet of resignation.

At seven o'clock the servant announced that the evening meal was ready, but Hasan could not eat. While Reza partook of a rice dish sprinkled with meat and fruit, the worried brother paced the floor. Once again he considered the possibilities. Perhaps Amin had been recognized . . . perhaps he had just been delayed . . . perhaps, perhaps . . .

"You should eat something Hasan," Reza said calmly, reaching for the tea. "There is nothing you can do now. Wherever Amin is, God is with him. It is hard to accept that your brother may be in peril, but there are times when all we can do is submit to our fate. This you should know from Ṭabarsí."

"Ṭabarsí was different." Hasan stopped pacing. "There, at least we could *act*. Fight! Here, I don't even know who or what the enemy is."

"Our faith is being tested, Hasan. The last two days have been hard on everyone, but we cannot allow it to overwhelm us. We have an obligation to our beloved Master. If we despair, then we have missed the real meaning of His great sacrifice."

While Reza spoke, Hasan again began to pace back and forth. "Perhaps I should go to the authorities."

"I don't think that would be wise." The older man realized that his friend had not been listening to his advice. "Questions would be asked, and the results could be disastrous for many people."

Hasan was just about to object when a knock at the door diverted his attention. Could it be Amin? Without thinking, he ran to the door and flung it open. The figure before him, however, was not his missing brother. It was Najaf-'Alí.

Courtesy dictated that Hasan invite the visitor to enter, but the disappointment of not seeing Amin's face caused him to forget his manners momentarily. For several seconds the two men stood and looked at each other in silence. It was only when Najaf-'Alí indicated, with a slight clearing of his throat, that he could not explain his call while standing outside that Hasan finally came to his senses. "Forgive me. I was hoping you were Amin. He has been missing since the morning. Come in. How are you?"

"To be honest, my dear friend, it is concerning Amín that I am here," declared Najaf-'Alí, after crossing the threshold.

"You mean you know where he is?"

"Yes." Najaf-'Alí's voice indicated that his news was not good. "He has been taken."

"It can't be," cried Reza, entering the passageway.

"It is true. He is being held in the very same barracks that housed our beloved Master, and . . ." For several seconds there was an ominous silence as Najaf-'Alí hesitated over the next, and most difficult part of his message. Finally he blurted out: "He is to be executed tomorrow morning."

Hasan could not believe what he was hearing. "That's impossible," he mumbled. "Completely impossible!"

Reza quickly recognized that Hasan was in a state of near shock and grabbed his hand. Calmly suggesting that they all go into the next room, he led his dazed friend through the velvet curtain and toward one of the large divans.

Once seated, Hasan's nerves began to quiet. "Do you know the charge?" he asked Najaf-'Alí.

"It appears he was publicly preaching the Báb's message. . . . The official charge will be the spreading of heretical doctrines; the same one for which our Lord was executed."

"He would not have done such a thing. Amín is not a fool."

"I am sure you are right," said Reza. "He certainly would have known that to do such a thing so close to the Master's execution would bring dire results."

"That may well be," continued Najaf-'Alí. "Still, the charge has been laid, and the sentence passed."

"Then it is hopeless?" Hasan's voice pleaded for a denial.

"As his closest relative you should be allowed a final visit," said the visitor. "I don't know what good it will do, but at least you might hear from Amin himself just what has happened."

"I will go," said Hasan slowly. "Who must I see?"

"A General Hulagu is in charge of the barracks where he is being kept. He will no doubt try to keep you away, so it may well take some time."

"Then I must leave now." Hasan stood up.

"I will accompany you as far as the citadel grounds," said Najaf-'Alí. "At night it is not easy to find."

After Hasan had found his shoes and put on his turban, the two men were ushered to the door by a reassuring Reza. "God will be with you Hasan," he said, "but this may help." Taking Hasan's hand, he thrust into it several silver coins and one gold *tumán*. Then opening the wooden portal he watched as the companions stepped out into the warm Tabriz night.

HASAN ARRIVED AT THE ARMY barracks two hours after sunset, but it was only much later that he was able to meet with General Hulagu. He almost failed to see the general at all, as the sentry on duty at first refused to grant his request. It was only after a lengthy discussion, and two of Reza's silver coins in hand, that the guard finally escorted him to the quarters of the commanding officer. Even when he found himself standing in front of the general, he was not sure if he would be allowed to stay, for the officer was by no means pleased with the late visit. "This is highly irregular," he snorted. "Highly irregular."

"Forgive me, sir," responded Hasan. "I only learned of my brother's arrest a few hours ago. If it is true that he is to be executed tomorrow, then I can only see him tonight."

"And how did you come to know of his arrest?" asked the general.

Hasan was about to mention Najaf-'Alí when he suddenly caught himself. Thinking quickly, he spat out in words the images that crossed his mind. "A . . . a friend of mine saw him being taken away from the court . . . and asked one of the guards."

"Hmm." The general gave Hasan a suspicious look. "And you know what the charge is?"

"No," Hasan lied.

"Heresy!" shouted the general. "Your brother is involved with this fanatical sect of Bábís."

Hulagu's explosion was followed by a period of silence as he rifled through the papers on his desk. Hasan attempted to formulate his next sentence, but his contemplation was interrupted when the general found what he was looking for. "Just as I thought," he said.

"What is it?" Hasan blurted out.

"I am afraid that it is impossible for you to see your brother without the consent of the Chief Lictor. He will not be available until tomorrow."

"But that could be too late," pleaded Hasan. "If I don't see him tonight, I might not be able to see him at all."

The general picked up a piece of paper from his desk. Carefully examining it, he began to think aloud. "The execution is to take place at eleven, and the Chief Lictor will be available at nine." Then letting go of the sheet, he brought his hands to his chin, propped his elbows on the table, and slowly rocked back and forth. "It would be highly irregular for me to allow you to see the prisoner without government permission. Furthermore, I have no proof that you are who you say you are."

"Ask me any question and check the answer with him," Hasan said quickly, perceiving a ray of hope.

"Unfortunately, he would tell us nothing. We don't even know his name."

Hasan's heart sank. It appeared that the general would not waver.

While Hulagu deliberately put his papers back into order, Hasan gathered his thoughts for a last emotional appeal. Just as the commander was about to motion for his orderly to show the visitor out, Hasan made his final bid. "Please understand my position, general. He is my younger brother, only nineteen years old. The rest of his family, his mother and his brothers, do not even know that he is here. It is a matter of family honor." Then Hasan reached down into his robe, removed the gold *tumán*, and carefully placed it on the general's desk. "It is all I have," he whispered.

Glancing at the gold, Hulagu sat back in his chair and tapped his fingers on the desk. "It would be highly irregular," he repeated, "highly irregular." Sitting forward, he became extremely serious. "You don't share his religious beliefs?"

The next moment seemed to Hasan like eternity. If he answered in the affirmative, he would not only be refused access to his brother, he would certainly endanger his own life and those of others. If he denied his belief, he would be recanting his faith. Finally, more out of instinct than rational reflection, he spit out his answer. "No!"

"Then curse the name of 'Alí-Muḥammad!" challenged the general.

There was no way out. Hasan wanted to jump up and grab the man by his neck, to squeeze the very life out of him. But he was trapped. With a tortured heart that he deceitfully covered with an emotionless face he said, "May 'Alí-Muḥammad and all who follow him burn in hell-fire."

"Well," cried the general with satisfaction, "it would be highly irregular—however, given your circumstances, I will allow you a short visit. Don't try anything, though. If you do, you will be sorry."

"Thank you, sir," Hasan mumbled, choking on his words.

General Hulagu arose from his desk, walked to the door, and yelled for the guard. "Take him to the cell of the young prisoner who was arrested this morning," the commander ordered. "Allow him twenty minutes—no more. Let him go in alone, but search him first. And keep the door bolted until they are finished."

The guard answered with a smart salute. The formalities over, the two men stepped out of the general's door and started back across the citadel square. After a few steps, the soldier halted, then turned to wait as Hasan placed the last two silver coins into his outstretched hand.

The distance from the general's quarters to the building that housed the prisoners' cells was about a hundred yards. Hasan passed the short journey deep in thought. He had spent so much of the last twelve hours thinking about how to find Amin that he had not considered what he would say to him once he had been located.

Still thinking how he would react, Hasan entered the cell block. Behind him the sentry watched his every move. As they proceeded along the dark and narrow corridor, the guard's glare became even more severe. Halfway down the passageway, they were met by another soldier.

As he walked, Hasan counted the heavy wooden doors on either side of the corridor. When he and his escorts came to a halt, they had arrived at the ninth cell. "Arms up," said one of the soldiers.

Turning toward his charge, the second guard briefly ran his hands over Hasan's robes. Finding nothing, he signaled his companion to open the cell door. After a moment or two of jostling with keys, the man thrust the appropriate one into the lock, freed the iron collar, and pushed the door open. Without hesitation, Hasan entered the dank cubicle. Behind him, the bolt clanged shut.

The room into which Hasan stepped was small, dark, and dirty. The distance from the door to the far wall could easily be covered in five paces, and the width of the cell was less than its length. It contained only a small dilapidated table and a half-burned candle whose flickering flame gave the cell its only light. There was no bed, no mattress or blanket on which Amin could lie, only the damp dirt floor.

Amin had been huddled in the far corner, but as Hasan entered the cell, he rose to his feet and staggered toward his brother. "Hasan," he cried, as they embraced. "How did you get in?"

"That is not important." Hasan held Amin tightly. "Are you all right?"

"As you can see, it isn't exactly one of Nematullah's guest rooms," Amin replied as he stepped back. "But I am alive."

"We were told you were openly preaching. Is it true?"

"No . . . unless speaking to my Beloved is considered such."

Puzzled, Hasan paused. "What do you mean?"

"I knew you would find it difficult to understand." Amin sat down against the wall and gestured to Hasan to do the same. "This morning I didn't go to the mosque as I told you, and I apologize for not speaking truthfully. Instead, I just walked, for miles, thinking. You see, yesterday, when I finally realized that His Holiness the Báb had been taken away from us, my belief began to founder —not in His Truth . . . rather, I think you might say, in God. I found that my feelings of anger and impotence had become shrouded in a black veil. The world, existence itself, seemed absurd."

Hasan listened intently. He had never heard Amin speak this way before. Now, as his ears were filled with his brother's words, he felt that the figure before him was mouthing thoughts that he had imagined were only his own.

"As I kept walking," Amin continued, "I plunged further and further into despondency. It seemed everything had fallen apart. Then it happened; I saw our Master. At first I thought I must be dreaming, but it was no vision. He was standing at the base of the citadel wall." Amin's eyes shone in the wavering light of the candle. "Hasan! At that instant my faith returned. I knew exactly what I had to do! I was to become a sacrifice for Him. In my grief, the Báb had bestowed His grace upon me."

"As Hasan listened to his brother, he realized that he faced a predicament. He had intended to suggest to Amin that he save his own life. Yet now the lad seemed convinced sacrifice was his destined mission. Any intimation from Hasan that he ignore the call would be immediately rejected. Still, Hasan felt he had to try to persuade his brother to change his mind. "I understand your commitment to the Master," he said cautiously. "But don't you think you would be of greater service to Him alive?"

Amin looked into Hasan's eyes. "It is out of my hands now. Don't you see? His Holiness has chosen me to do His will. Would you have me renounce Him?"

"What about the family?" implored Hasan, his voice quickening to match his racing pulse. "Mother will be distraught, and Nematullah will be beside himself."

"They will come to accept it. God will certainly soothe their pain."

For the second time that day, a feeling of helplessness descended on Hasan. He wanted to take his brother by the shoulders and shake him violently. Yet Amin's faith was so sincere that it could not but elicit his respect. Caught in this dilemma, Hasan could only sit quietly and allow the conflicting emotions to do battle in his already fatigued mind.

Recognizing his brother's perplexity, Amin tried to calm him. "It has all become very clear to me, my dear Hasan," he said softly. "I had often wondered about those mysterious events in Shiraz when I first had the privilege of meeting our Lord: the strange dream, the messenger, the Master's Tablet. And then, our escape from Ṭabarsí. Why was my life spared, when men of such nobility as Quddús and Mullá Ḥusayn were taken? Now I know, Hasan! I know that it was all for a purpose—so that I might be sacrificed on the same spot where our Beloved Báb gave His life. For some undeserved reason, God has chosen me to demonstrate to the people of this city that our faith in the Master has not been extinguished."

As he spoke, tears of joy began to roll down Amin's

cheeks, and Hasan also felt his own eyes filling. Fighting off the emotional surge within, he found enough control to ask his final question. "Amin, is there nothing that can change your mind?"

Amin gently touched his brother's arm. "Don't be sad, Hasan," he whispered. "It is a joyous event. Be happy for me."

As Hasan looked at his brother, he heard footsteps in the corridor. The full force of the realization hit him. This would be the last time he would ever see Amin's face. He studied it like an artist preparing to paint a portrait, concentrating on every feature, noticing every line.

The pounding of the guard's fist on the door interrupted his thoughts. "Time to go," said a rough voice. The door was unbolted. Hasan reached out to embrace his brother. It was all too much for him. Tears rushed down his face in a torrent. "Amin!" he sobbed.

"All will be well, Hasan," Amin assured him. "Paradise awaits me."

The impatient guard grabbed the back of Hasan's robe and pulled him away. "Move," he yelled. "Your time is up."

Hasan took a last look at his brother. Then suddenly he was in the passageway and the door was slammed shut.

Chapter 16

HASAN SAT ALONE on the rooftop of Mírzá Reza's house. Above him, the stars sparkled brightly, seeming to dance in the clearness of the warm midnight sky. It had been over three days now since his brother's execution. Still he found himself incapable of action. He had not yet informed the family of Amin's death, nor had he followed Reza's advice and taken any of his meals. During the past seventy-two hours, only a few swallows of tea had passed his lips.

When he had left the prison several nights before, he thought he had come to terms with Amin's sacrifice. The young man had shown such profound faith that it was infectious. Although he was deeply saddened by his departure, Hasan had felt a sense of inner quiet. As the hour of the execution grew nearer, however, his doubts had returned, and he had become despondent. The hour came and went, but Hasan remained inside the house. Except for short excursions to the rooftop, he had not left the building since.

Now, as his eyes searched the starry heavens, a variety of emotions swirled through his soul. Into the great void which Amin's death had created rushed feelings of loss, anger, guilt, and despair. Amin had been so much a part of him that he now found it difficult to accept that he was gone.

In fact, he knew that he had not accepted it. How, he kept wondering, could anything so real, so meaningful, cease to be? How is it that our present vanishes? The very rooftop on which he was sitting—was it real? It too would cease to exist some day. Yet now, at this instant, such a thought seemed ridiculous. It was here: solid and strong. In the same way, he knew that he had not yet accepted Amin's death. Only four nights ago he had touched him, seen his smile, heard his voice. How could all of that become nothing?

Streams of sweat rolled down his forehead and his hands became moist. For the next half hour he fought with his feelings. Then, in an attempt to will away his loss, he returned to the past. He closed his eyes and allowed his mind to wander freely. He remembered their childhood together: Amin, always obedient, the ideal child. He had always been the first to say his prayers, complete his chores, and finish his work, which made him the jewel of his parents' eyes. Even Nematullah, the eldest son, did not receive the praise reserved for Amin.

One after another the images appeared. There was Amin at his fifteenth birthday: strong, handsome, childlike in his simplicity. Then he was working in the shop; unrolling and measuring yards of cloth with a devotion that verged on the religious. Next, his face at the barricade walls at Ṭabarsí; firm and devout, despite hunger and fatigue. And finally, in his prison cell: joyful in his victorious faith.

As these thoughts passed through his mind, Hasan began to feel a change in himself. From a mood of nostalgic reflection, he found himself giving in to feelings of anger: anger at himself for the things he had left undone— the time he had wasted, which might have been spent in meaningful communion with Amin; anger at his older brother Nematullah for his lack of understanding; anger at the mullás for their hypocritical pretensions; anger at the government leaders, those beasts of prey who gloried in their war making. And finally, an undefined anger at life itself. How could a man be asked to love a life that offered up such enticements, only to have them snatched away? . . . And now he realized that he was uttering blasphemy.

But there was no stopping the flow of passion that swept his being. Like flashes of cannon fire, life's absurdities shot to the forefront of his consciousness. The mounds of human skulls which every schoolboy learned of—skulls left behind by the invading Mongols who had ravaged the country centuries before. What innocent suffering lay buried in those piles of bone? Why was evil so often rewarded, while truth and honesty were trampled into the dust of history? How did such an atrocity fit into the scheme of things? Could God in his omnipotence have prevented it? Was it, as the mullás claimed, an expression of God's wrath toward men for not recognizing the Imams?

His mind wanted to rest, but it was pushed on by its own momentum. He saw the poverty and squalor of thousands of peasants who had lost their livelihood to flood and drought, were bled dry by those like his brother. And the poor of the cities, living in the shadows of mosques whose elegant domes bespoke God's glory: how they would throw themselves down on their knees five times a day while their children ran through the dusty alleyways shoeless and covered with dirt and filth! If they were fortunate, they might receive alms; if not . . .

To these questions was added the whole problem of religious knowledge: the one Nematullah had raised months earlier. Was it not absurd to think of God as asking man— imperfect, ignorant man—to know *Truth* and then judge him for his failure to do so? Perhaps if it were a question of black and white—but life was never black and white.

Many great men had refused to follow the Prophets. Were they less pious than the pretentious mullás who took it upon themselves to carry out the Prophet's will? What of false prophets? How was a man to know if a claim was true? In such a system, God became the grand magician who, like the sleight-of-hand artist at the bazaar, delighted in the fact that his audience could not select the golden nugget. Then there was the hidden Imam: Men were asked to believe that for centuries a divinely appointed spokesman had remained suspended in time, only to reappear at the end of history—the absurdity of absurdities. No wonder that the man who claimed this station was put to death and his followers hunted down as if they were madmen.

The more Hasan thought, the greater became his disdain, and the more pahtetic seemed the human condition. And what was more pathetic than his own predicament? He had denied his own faith and wished for his brother to do the same. And for what? A few extra years in a world that was only worthy of scorn.

He was caught; he knew it. His mind had locked him in a corner. He could not escape his own cowardliness. He could not love God. His only hope was action: some deed that would express his new feeling of universal contempt. Unexpectedly it came to him. A sense of relief swept through his being. Again he turned and looked at the sky. "So vast," he whispered, "so vast." Rising to his feet, he started toward the stairway and the house below.

Chapter 17

FAINT STREAKS OF LIGHT broke through the patchwork of clouds that dotted the horizon. For the two men crouched in the heavy underbrush, the night had passed slowly, and with the first signs of dawn their spirits were lifted. They both realized that soon their goal would be accomplished.

The thicket lay at the foot of a small hill, one of the several which distinguished the royal hunting grounds from the remainder of the rolling tableland. Beside it ran a small, twisting stream, whose clear water trickled slowly over time-worn pebbles in a gentle but continuous gargle. Beyond the stream lay a broad, grassy meadow, spotted with wildflowers. To the south, the meadow opened into an undulating plain, while to the north, just up the hill from where the men were concealed, ran a narrow dirt road which led from a small hamlet to the army encampment and palace grounds of Níyávarán.

"It shouldn't be much longer now," said Ṣádiq-i Tabrízí, turning to his companion. "Soon he will leave the encampment and come down the road for his morning promenade. If all goes well, our plans should be realized within the hour."

The man who spoke was dressed in a dull brown robe that blended in well with the surrounding thicket. Slightly built, with pointed features that suggested a peasant ancestry, his appearance did not give the impression of power or strength, but his fiery spirit more than made up for his lack of physical size. Like most Persian men his age, he wore a full beard. After a long and restless night in the underbrush, it was speckled with green and yellow grass. Turbanless out of choice rather than necessity, his short-cropped black hair showed signs of losing its youthful thickness. If one looked closely, it was evident that his hairline was starting to recede.

"You are sure this is the place, Ṣádiq?" asked his comrade, Fatḥu'lláh-i Qumí.

"Of course," Ṣádiq answered sharply. "Many times my father brought me her to see the shah. He admired the royal family and never missed an opportunity to see them."

"That must have been some time ago," said Fatḥu'lláh.

"Yes, my friend, it was years ago, but the promenade is a tradition that all sovereigns follow. Náṣiri'd-Dín will certainly do the same."

Firm in the assurance that his companion's prediction was correct, Fatḥu'lláh lay back in the underbrush to wait. Like Ṣádiq, he was slight of build and youthfully vigorous. Yet whereas his companion seemed obsessed by his mission, Fatḥu'lláh was still capable of lighthearted jest, a trait which often annoyed his more serious accomplice. He too wore a brown robe, although slightly darker in color than Ṣádiq's, and his head was covered with a turban whose color exactly matched that of his garment.

From his position several hundred yards up the roadway, Hasan could faintly see the figures of the two men with whom he had come to Níyávarán. Like them, he had spent the night in the brush, but his assignment required he take a position much closer to the royal encampment. While he felt isolated, he realized the necessity of his role and carried it out with no sign of animosity or complaint.

As he alternated his glance between the thicket and the entryway to the palace grounds, Hasan recalled the origin

162

of the plot that had brought them here. Following the death of the Báb, he had heard rumors of an attempt to be made on the life of the shah. Although he had not initially sought out the conspirators, he could not help being drawn to their idea. After Amin had been executed and the bottom had fallen out of his life, he had remembered them. Despite the fact that he knew such an attempt was completely against the wishes of the Bábí community's leaders, his need for revenge caused him to call on one of the conspirators to probe the seriousness of their intentions. As it turned out, Ṣádiq-i Tabrízí had personal reasons for wanting the shah dead. Not only was he despondent over the Báb's execution, like Hasan he had tasted the bitterness of personal loss. His closest friend had been felled by the bullets of imperial troops. Both men agreed that only the death of the sovereign, the symbol of power and authority, would satisfy their deepest inner desires.

Two years had now passed since that fateful night. Numerous plans had been made and set into motion. But, time and again, unforeseen circumstances had forced them to be abandoned. At one time Hasan had even come to feel that their schemes and designs would never come to fruition. Now, however, as he sat in his lookout perch peering down at the roadway beneath him, it seemed that the object for which they had waited would finally be attained.

While Hasan reflected about the past, Ṣádiq and Fatḥu' lláh were busy discussing the present. Although Ṣádiq had reviewed the plan many times, he felt it necessary to repeat the details yet again. This was his way: serious and thorough. "And make sure you look inconspicuous," he growled at his companion. "Whatever you do, keep your pistol well concealed under your cloak."

His own mention of firearms momentarily diverted Ṣádiq's thought. He glanced quickly into Fatḥu'lláh's eyes. "You are sure that the guns are good? You have loaded them well?"

"I have taken care of everything," Fatḥu'lláh assured him. "Don't worry; all will go well."

Half an hour passed before the first of the local townfolk began to arrive, and it was not long until large groups of people could be seen converging upon the area. They lined the roadway on either side anxiously hoping to catch a glimpse of their ruler. In the thicket below, Ṣádiq and Fatḥu'lláh could only hear their excitement, whereas Hasan felt the full visual impact of their presence. In both cases, however, the men experienced a surge of energy as the anticipated moment grew ever closer. On Ṣádiq's forehead, sweat beads began to gather. Fatḥu'lláh tried to busy himself by silently fiddling with his hands. As for Hasan, the pace of his alternating glances between the thicket and the roadway began to accelerate dramatically.

Then he saw what he was looking for. Coming into view from behind a clump of trees that marked the entryway into the palace encampment were a large number of horses on which were seated sword-bearing guardsmen. Behind them, adorned in royal blue, and wearing the traditional military headpiece of the monarchy, was the shah himself, Náṣiri'd-Dín. Rhythmically bouncing atop his cantering black steed, his chest projecting outward from his upright body, he appeared unconcerned with those around him. Indeed, so high was his chin that had his guards decided to abandon him, he would probably not have noticed.

As the party swung slowly around and straightened itself onto the roadway, the crowd began to buzz. For a moment Hasan became lost in the festive pageantry. Quickly taking hold of himself, however, he grabbed for the small white cloth he had carefully concealed inside his robe. Raising it to shoulder level, he dropped it on the ground.

"There's the signal." Ṣádiq had spotted the fluttering cloth. *"Bismilláh.* May God protect us."

Fatḥu'lláh scrambled to his feet. Stuffing his pistol into his robe, he followed Ṣádiq out of the thicket and up the hill.

While the two men hurried through the underbrush, Hasan looked back at the oncoming train. Although he was now supposed to descend the hill and gather the concealed horses, he tarried momentarily to gaze at the image before him. There he was: the Shahanshah—the King of Kings—who traced the glory of his title back twenty-four hundred years; the shah, whose might and authority was unquestioned; the shah, who resided in magnificent palaces; the shah, almost a god on earth. He turned in disgust and made his way toward the waiting horses.

Just as Hasan had begun to carry out his duty, Ṣádiq and Fatḥu'lláh reached the top of the hill. Brushing away the pieces of grass which stuck to their robes, the two men paused before moving toward the roadway. Although the two figures looked out of place as they wandered down the sloping ridge, the crowd was by this time absorbed by the spectacle of the shah's appearance. No one noticed that the men had not come from the town.

"There is the place," declared Ṣádiq, pointing to a small garden on the other side of the roadway. "Here we part. Qásim will be waiting for you."

"Right," said Fatḥu'lláh, still panting. Taking several deep breaths, he left Ṣádiq for the spot directly across from the garden. He had only traveled a few yards when he saw Qásim. The large-framed, gray-turbaned accomplice was standing motionless behind a group of spectators. Turning his walk into a near-run, he joined the other man.

Seconds later, Ṣādiq arrived at the entrance of the garden. He pushed his way to the front of a small gate, stopped, and peered across the roadway. With a brisk wave of his hand he indicated to his two companions that all was ready and leaned back against the wooden barrier to wait.

Now that they were in position, Ṣādiq breathed easier. The royal party was now negotiating a sharp turn in the road, a maneuver which provided him with an excellent side view of its formation. He studied it with the intensity of a skilled hunter. At the head of the column were the usual lance-carrying equerries, followed closely by a number of grooms whose prancing horses were covered with intricately patterned, jewel-studded blankets. Behind them rode the nomadic cavalry, their rifles slung boldly over their shoulders and their swords hanging freely from their saddles. A small gap separated this vanguard from the royal retinue proper, whose lords, chiefs, and officers —all dressed in their finest military apparel—preceded by a short distance the figure whom thousands of stretching necks strained to see.

Perfect, thought Ṣādiq. It couldn't be better. The shah is virtually isolated. All we have to do is wait for the retinue to pass and we will have a clear view.

The regal procession made its way around the bend in the road and then straigthened up for the last leg of the journey to the parade ground. As the distance between themselves and the first horses shortened, the accomplices could feel their pulses quicken. By the time the lancers were upon them, it was as if their hearts had become bass drums. The time of reckoning was near.

When the shah was a few feet away, Ṣádiq gave his signal. All at once, the three men moved forward and threw themselves to the ground. "We are your sacrifice," they cried out in unison. "We humbly make a request."

Hearing the traditional greeting, the shah first thought that the men were just over-zealous commoners. Only when their call was followed by another sudden movement in his direction was he taken aback. "What do you want, you rascals?" he shouted. "Get away!"

By this time, all three men had drawn their weapons. As the shah gasped in fright, Ṣádiq grabbed the reins of his horse and attempted to pull him off course. Reacting violently, the sovereign kicked out at his assailant. "Get away, demons!" he yelled.

Ṣádiq answered the royal command with a shot from his gun. And no sooner had their leader discharged his weapon than Fatḥu'lláh and Qásim followed suit. One burst cut the collar of precious pearls adorning the royal horse's neck, while another flew off harmlessly into the air. Only Ṣádiq hit his target, riddling Náṣiri'd-Dín's arm and back with buckshot. But the force of the discharge was so weak that it barely wounded the sovereign.

"You fool!" Ṣádiq shouted. "Fatḥu'lláh, you miserable fool, you loaded the pistols with buckshot!" Throwing his gun to the ground, Ṣádiq grabbed the shah's leg. His two accomplices also attacked the royal personage, but the wild wheeling of the horse, and the rapid blows which they received from the fists of the frightened king, prevented them from unseating him. Even though Ṣádiq had responded to the initial failure by unsheathing his dagger, the delay their miscalculation had caused brought doom upon the assassins. The royal retinue, which at first had been thrown into consternation by the assault on their king, now hurried to his aid. The hapless attackers were soon surrounded by a sea of angry soldiers. Within seconds, Ṣádiq fell to the slash of a nomad's sword. Almost simultaneously Fatḥu'lláh and Qásim were wrestled to the ground by members of the royal guard.

From his position in the gully below, Hasan heard the guns go off. In his mind he fantasized about the stricken look on the dying shah's face. When after several minutes, however, he saw no one come running down the hill, he left the horses and charged up to the summit. Everywhere he looked, man and beast were in motion. In the middle of the bedlam lay his three companions: Fatḥu'lláh and Qásim heavily bound with rope, and Ṣádiq, already lifeless, hanging from the back of a mule.

Watching from afar, Hasan was pulled in two directions. His heart told him that he should rush to the aid of his fallen comrades; his head dictated against such a move, since there could be no hope of freeing them. For a long moment this conflict of soul tore him. Was it cowardice that had kept him alive—that always told him to flee? Should he not throw reason to the wind and charge forward to a glorious death? This surge of emotion almost controlled him, and he was about to urge his horse forward when his sanity again returned. "I would not give them the satisfaction," he whispered. Swinging his animal back toward the gully, he galloped off, praying that the consequences of their failure would not be too horrible.

Chapter 18

Mírzá Áqá K͟hán sat silently on the finely woven, blue and white Isfahan carpet spread before the royal dais. In front of him was a large silver tray filled with fruit, from which he chose piece after piece of fresh melon. He was a man of small stature with features that immediately impressed any visitor to the royal court as forbidding: narrow chin, bony nose, solemn, if not resentful, eyes. Although he was attired in a silk robe, there was no doubt in the minds of those who knew him that he paid more attention to the duties of his office than to his fancy paraphernalia. Indeed, it was commonly felt in the capital that it was his utter seriousness, his almost religious devotion to the throne, that had caused Náṣiri'd-Dín to raise him to the highest position in the land following the death of the former vizier, Mírzá Taqí K͟hán, at the hands of an assassin in the baths at Fin. And now, as he sat waiting for his king to arrive, this devotion took the form of schemes designed to eliminate the followers of the Báb.

The minister's wait was short. From the far end of the spacious hall, the clatter of feet announced the arrival of the King of Kings. He was accompanied by a flock of attendants, four of whom carried him in a sedan chair. Although it had been three days since the attack, the shah was still weak. Despite the fact that his bandages were well concealed by his gold and blue blouse, the stiffness with which he held his upper body indicated that his wounds were still causing him discomfort.

As soon as the train entered the room, Mírzá Áqá K͟hán

rose to his feet. Along with the other courtiers, he listened reverently as the herald loudly proclaimed the sovereign's virtues. "The most august, the most brave, the most virtuous Náṣiri'd-Dín is now present. May we all be thankful for his life."

While the imperial party made its way down the hallway, men dropped and touched their heads to the floor, acknowledging that they were in the presence of God's representative on earth. Apparently unmoved by this show of devotion, Náṣiri'd-Dín looked ahead, impatient to reach his destination. When the party finally arrived at the foot of the throne, he ordered the attendants to lower the chair. As they did so, another member of the entourage stepped forward to help the monarch descend. But Náṣiri'd-Dín waved the servant away and stepped out unassisted onto the polished marble floor. Once on his feet, he slowly and hesitantly ascended the stairs leading to the velvet-cushioned throne. When he reached the top of the dais, he turned toward his audience, scanned the hall, and then seated himself, trying as best he could to maintain a look of royal dignity.

For the next hour the shah received courtiers, heard petitions, and signed royal decrees. All the while, Mírzá Áqá Khán remained seated on the carpet, giving no indication that he was concerned with the events taking place around him. Beneath the aloof exterior, however, he was anxious for the proceedings to be concluded so he could be alone with the monarch. Still, he knew that the ceremony had to go on. Thus he did all he could to appear unperturbed.

When the final request had been granted and the hall was clear of petitioners, the shah turned wearily to his prime minister. "You desire to see me?"

Mírzá Áqá Khán stood up and deliberately approached the foot of the dais. "Yes, Your Majesty." He lowered his head as a mark of official respect.

"What is it that concerns you?"

"I do not like to remind your majesty of the terrible events of several days ago," the Prime Minister said, "but certain information has come to us regarding the source of the plot to take your life."

Hearing these words, the shah straightened his shoulders and leaned forward. "Yes?" he said, grimacing slightly from the pain that the movement produced.

Mírzá Áqá Khán took note of his master's interest and went on. "We know, as your mother believed, that the followers of Sayyid 'Alí-Muḥammad, the Báb, were behind the attempted assassination."

"Has the prisoner talked?" The shah's eyes became suddenly more intense.

"No, he still refuses to say anything, but a very reliable informant has told us that he is a disciple of the dead heretic."

The shah sat back in his chair. Resting his head against the purple velvet cushion that adorned the top of his throne, he concentrated on the words his minister had just spoken. Then, his voice rising in pitch, he gave vent to his growing frustration. "I thought that the death of that man would put an end to the activities of these fanatics. His execution was supposed to demonstrate the falsity of his claims. Instead, his followers seem to be increasing daily and causing more trouble than ever."

The vizier could see that his master was becoming anxious. "Ever since the Báb was executed, the impact of the movement has declined dramatically," he said. "It is certainly true that there still remains an active handful of fanatics whose tenacity we have perhaps misjudged . . . but we can solve this problem." Mírzá Áqá Khán had thrown out the bait. Now he waited for the sovereign's response.

"And what do you plan to do?" came the expected question.

"We have arrested a number of their most ardent believers. Let us charge them with plotting to take the life of the king and execute them, in the manner of criminals, in Your Majesty's presence. Furthermore, I would ask you to sign a royal decree calling for the immediate arrest of all known adherents of this dreadful heresy."

"My father put an end to the practice of royal executions. A sudden return to this practice would cause consternation in many circles."

"Your father was not attacked by a group of heretical fanatics," shot back the Prime Minister. "It must be made clear that the Crown will not tolerate an attack on its honor."

"Could we not just execute the ones we have captured? Why must we kill men who were not involved in the attempt?"

"Because this movement must be stamped out. This will not only demonstrate to the entire realm the sedition and disloyalty at the core of these infidel beliefs, it will symbolize our attitude toward anyone associated with them. In other words, from a practical point of view, it is the best deterent we have. A royal execution has a power which affects all men."

The shah looked away. The idea of a royal execution instinctively repelled him. But if it were to put an end to the threats on his life? Perhaps the Prime Minister was right? "Who are these men you have arrested?" he asked finally, delaying his decision.

"As I said earlier," replied Mírzá Áqá Khán, "they are some of the sect's most zealous converts. Most of them are merchants, an occupation in which the movement seems to abound.

Once more the shah paused and systematically considered his minister's request. "And when do you propose that the executions take place?"

"Tomorrow morning."

"So soon?"

Recognizing apprehension in the shah's voice, Mírzá Áqá Khán hurriedly began to explain. "It is important that the impact of a royal execution be made as soon as possible. I have been told by reliable sources that these rebels will not stop until they have gained their objective—Your Majesty's death."

The Prime Minister had been driven to his final resort. By lying to the shah he hoped to play on the sovereign's fears and get the decision he wanted. He had used this ploy many times in the past, and would no doubt use it again if he felt it necessary. Now he waited, hoping that Náṣiri'd-Dín would yield.

"All right," said the shah hesitantly, "if it must be."

Mírzá Áqá Khán gave an inner sigh of relief. He lowered his head almost to his knees. "Your Royal Majesty is most wise."

"You are a faithful servant," replied Náṣiri'd-Dín.

THE NEXT MORNING Mírzá Áqá Khán ordered the prisoners to be brought up from the dungeons below the royal palace to their place of execution—the same hall where only hours earlier the vizier had convinced the monarch of his scheme. The scene that awaited them, however, was much different from the one which visiting courtiers had seen the day

173

before. While the shah and his throne still dominated the setting, the area just in front of the dais was covered with a small wooden platform which stretched fifteen feet in either direction. On two sides of the platform stood a large crowd of onlookers especially chosen by the Prime Minister. Those who had the best view were dignitaries and members of the court, while minor officials and privileged commoners stood behind.

The nature of the fate toward which the bound men were headed had been designed by Mírzá Áqá Khán to elicit the response he so badly wanted. The executions were to be divided among different departments of the government. The shah would come first, but to save the dignity of the Crown, the Steward of the Household would act as the sovereign's representative and fire the shot. Executioners would then be drawn from the secretariat, foreign ministry, and so on, until all the branches of government had taken their turn. The ulama, the merchants, the artillery, and the infantry would likewise be given a Bábí. To maintain variety in the proceedings and keep the spectators amused, a different method of capital punishment was to be alloted to each new dignitary who took the stage.

As the men were brought into the hall, a hush fell over the assemblage. What they saw, however, soon unsettled them. Rather than cowering and fearful figures, the Bábís before them were defiant and clearly unafraid. Despite the guards' repeated orders for silence, they filled the air with a resounding verbal assault.

Seething with anger, Mírzá Áqá Khán confronted the group as they approached the platform and struck the closest of the prisoners on the side of the head. "Even at the hour of your death you would show no remorse!" he screamed.

The man lifted his head and turned his face toward the

Prime Minister. His dark brown eyes stared into those of his persecutor. "Did the Imám Ḥusayn show remorse at Karbala?" he answered.

Mírzá Áqá Khán was beside himself with rage. Grabbing the man by his robe, the Prime Minister flung him in the direction of the platform, his fury giving him the strength that his size could not. "This is a so-called man of God," he yelled, addressing the shah and the assembled guests. "Not only does he plot against his sovereign, he blasphemes the holy Imam."

Mírzá Áqá Khán signaled to the Steward of the Household to carry out his assignment. While sovereign and subjects looked on, the red-robed courtier stepped foward and unloaded his firearm at point blank range. The sudden burst of gunfire caused most of the spectators to jump back in fright. They hardly noticed that in spite of the close range at which he was firing, the steward had not dispatched his victim, but merely wounded him by blowing off his ear. It was only the shouts of praise to his Beloved that made them realize that the blood-covered man was not dead. "Happy is he who is smote by the infidel's sword. In the path of the Qá'im, he will gladly sacrifice all."

Almost unable to believe his eyes, the Prime Minister turned to the bare-chested swordsman standing beside him and gestured to the man to finish the deed. While the victim continued to shout, the executioner jumped onto the platform. After mumbling a short invocation to Allah, he raised his sword. Swiftly pulling the blade down, he struck the man squarely on the back of the neck, neatly severing the now turbanless head from his body.

The job accomplished, the swordsman looked victoriously at Mírzá Áqá Khán, but the latter's gaze was directed toward the rest of the prisoners. Rather than expressing fear at the sight of their decapitated companion, they continued to defy their captors. Two of the men began to sing benedictions to the Báb. Another twirled in dervish fashion, repeating the names of God. Others shouted at the Prime Minister words which indicated that it was he who had betrayed 'Alí and the Imams.

Amid this turmoil, Mírzá Áqá Khán glanced at the shah. The monarch's eyes told him what he feared: his cramped lips and furrowed brow testified to his growing displeasure. The Prime Minister instinctively knew that if something were not done to put an end to the growing confusion, grave consequences would follow. Accordingly, he rushed toward the singing prisoners, hastily waving directions to the assigned executioners lining the far side of the platform. He yelled at the guards to deliver the victims to the stage. One by one, the enraptured followers of the Báb were thrown forward to meet their end—some by pistols, some by daggers and swords, and still others by more ingenious weapons, such as hatchets and maces. However, through it all, the tenacity of the Bábís did not waver. By the time the last of the prisoners had taken his place on the blood-soaked and body-strewn stage, the mood of the guests had changed. Instead of the scoffing and jeering which had accompanied the first executions, the hall was infused with a haunting stillness, a silence which was only interrupted by the words of the last victim. "In the chambers of the shah," he shouted to the crowd, "you have witnessed the shame of Islam. May God have mercy on you."

The mullá who was assigned the last Bábí gave no time for the spectators to respond. Swinging an ax with all the force he could muster, he cracked open the skull of the defiant heretic and drove him to the ground. At once, a blue-coated cavalry officer rushed to the body. Drawing his sword, he completed the ritual by hacking off the man's head.

The performance complete, Mírzá Áqá K͟hán turned to salute his sovereign. His gesture was brought to a sudden halt by the shah himself, who, rising from his throne, descended unannounced down the dais steps. Before leaving, he stopped before the Prime Minister. "This is your idea of royal prestige?" he said in a trembling voice. "It is nothing but a mockery." Without waiting for a reply he threw his hands into the air and made his way through the prostrate crowd.

Still flushed, the vizier turned to follow the shah. "Clear the hall," he shouted to the guards. "See to it that this mess is cleaned up." Then he hurried after his disgruntled monarch.

Chapter 19

Mírzá Reza gently pushed back the velvet curtain that separated the main visiting area from the rest of the house and wended his way down the hallway toward Hasan's room. Entering the doorway, he announced his arrival with a loud, purposeful command. "Make sure that your things are ready. It is only a few hours now."

Hasan looked up at his friend. "I don't know if I should go," he said in a dejected voice.

"Don't be foolish," barked Reza. "You know how serious the situation is. Or don't you believe the stories of the arrests and executions? There is really no choice—you must leave with us tonight."

"It isn't that I don't understand." Hasan looked away from Reza. "I just feel that perhaps I shouldn't run. I am thinking of turning myself in."

Reza's eyes widened in disbelief. "Do you know what you are saying? Have you any idea what they would do to you? What the others received would seem merciful compared to what would happen now that Mírzá Áqá Khán is on the rampage."

A series of rapid knocks halted Reza's admonishment.

"I will see who it is." Quickly he returned to the hallway.

"My dear Mírzá Rahim," he said as he opened the door. "Please come in."

From the turbulent expression on Rahim's face, Reza could tell that the call was not a casual one. Not bothering to inquire about his visitor's health, he ushered the black-robed man in. "What is it, my friend?"

"The order has arrived from the capital that all known followers of the Báb are to be arrested," Rahim stammered. "And they have already taken a large number of believers into custody. From what I can gather, thirty or forty men were rounded up during the night, including Dasturi and many of his friends. It is said that they will be taken to Tehran and put in the Síyáh Chál."

"My dear God," Reza groaned. "The Black Pit. To think of men chained in that foul place. How did you come to know of Dasturi's arrest?"

"We share the same physician, the Austrian doctor Menzel. He was at Dasturi's house when the authorities came. Being a Christian, he was not molested. I saw him this morning and he informed me."

"So it has come to this," whispered Reza, covering his face in despair.

"They want to exterminate us."

"We must leave tonight. Even one day's delay could be catastrophic."

Reza uncovered his face. "I am having trouble with Hasan," he said bluntly. "He was saying something just now about turning himself in to the authorities."

"He can't be serious! You must talk to him. Whatever you do, don't let him surrender himself. It would be a disaster. Not only for him, but for all of us. You must persuade him to leave with us tonight. We don't need any more martyrs."

"I will do my best," said Reza. "But, as you know, he is a very strong-willed man. It is both his strength and his weakness.

Rahim turned to leave. "We will be here at midnight," he said emphatically. "Be ready, for time is precious."

"*We* will be ready."

"Good; and now I must go."

"Take care, my friend. May God be with you."

Rahim was already moving toward the door. Without further exchange, Reza saw his friend out into the night.

Now that Mírzá Rahim was gone, Reza closed the door and started back to Hasan's room. After taking only a few steps, he stopped. What should I say to him, he thought. How can I have any influence on his decision?

While Reza reflected on the task before him, Hasan sat on the edge of his chair, peering down at the floor. He had overheard Rahim's remarks and knew that Reza would soon arrive in the doorway. A man with good intentions, he mused. But he would never understand.

"I know what you are thinking," said Reza, entering the room. "I don't want to lecture you, yet I feel that a rash decision might later be regretted."

"I rarely do anything rash. I have given the situation much thought: perhaps too much thought."

"Then why could you possibly want to stay?" insisted Reza. "Especially now, when they are arresting our friends in Tabriz. Mírzá Rahim just—"

"I heard what Mírzá Rahim said."

"Then you will know how serious the situation is," continued Reza without breaking stride. "Certainly we are admonished not to fear death, but there is much work to do for this Cause. And it can only be done by the living."

Hasan took a deep breath. Reza had hit upon the real issue, and now that the door was open, he knew that he must answer in full. "You see, my friend," he began, "I don't think I can serve this Cause. I have lost my faith. Or perhaps to be more accurate, I now know that I never had faith. Amin was different: he loved the Báb with a rare spiritual passion. But as for me, I never felt as he did.

When I journeyed to Badasht to join him, it was from a sense of disillusionment—and perhaps a love for Amin himself—not from any true commitment to the Master. Yes, there were times—especially at the conference—when I was moved. I felt that I could really believe in this Qá'im. But those feelings never took root. I was hoping, not believing.''

Momentarily the flow of words ceased, as Hasan tried desperately to order his mind. At the same time, Reza could see that his friend was struggling. Looking toward the other side of the room, he remained silent.

"After Amin was arrested," Hasan finally continued, "in fact, the night before his execution, I finally began to think more about myself and my part in the community. And I came to realize that I had joined this Cause more for Amin than for Sayyid-i Báb, or God. I had no real faith. That very evening I had been willing to curse the name of my Master and had tried to get Amin to do the same. Then when he was gone I seemed to lose all purpose. There was a void. I felt angry; I felt hypocritical. And I responded the way I have always responded: I acted. Now my actions have brought more pain and suffering. I feel like I am against a wall. Maybe the only solution is to follow Amin's footsteps. Maybe only death can give my life any meaning.''

There was a dominating silence. Hasan had emptied himself in one large geyser-gush and was now speechless. Reza could not marshal his own thoughts into any coherent pattern.

"That kind of death will not give your life meaning," Mírzá Reza said finally. "I admit that I do not understand your feelings. But you are mistaken if you think that capitulation will bring justification. If it has any result at all, it will be to undermine any meaning your life may have held. You would be turning your back on all those who gave up their lives at Ṭabarsí. You would be affirming that Amin's life was sacrificed in vain."

Reza looked at Hasan, hoping for a response. When he did not get one, he spoke again. "I do not mean to be harsh, Hasan. But I believe what I said is true. Your crisis of faith is no doubt genuine, and I sympathize with you. Your solution, however, will not resolve the problem facing you. Amin, those hundreds of men at Ṭabarsí—they all died for *something*. You would be dying for nothing. Death can only have meaning if it is sacrificial. The death you propose is not a sacrifice—it is a surrender: surrender not only to the mullás and their hypocrisy, but surrender to meaninglessness, and to despair. I am sorry. Such a death would only be cowardice."

Although he had planned to deliver his second speech with more control, Reza had once again raised his voice to a passionate pitch. Now, after releasing his feelings of frustration, only to experience the aftershocks of guilt and remorse, he realized the nature of his over-zealous posture. Turning sheepishly away from Hasan, he said no more.

Hasan, meanwhile, painfully struggled with the sermon his friend had just delivered. The word *cowardice* rang through his mind, and pangs of conscience struck him as they had after the failure at Níyávarán. He had not considered his decision in such terms. In fact, he had thought that, by turning himself in and admitting his complicity in the assassination attempt, he would be demonstrating his bravery. Now he was forced to reevaluate his position. He could not but respect Reza for his truthfulness. I have misjudged him, he thought.

Having taken the first step of admitting to himself the weakness of his own position, Hasan allowed the implications of this insight to sink in. Before many more seconds had passed, he looked up at Reza and made his confession. "You are right, my friend. I may have no faith, but I will not surrender."

Reza smilcd. "God is the judge of faith," he said. "Prepare your things. We leave at midnight."

Chapter 20

A SHARP, STABBING PAIN in his left arm woke Hasan with a start. For a moment he forgot where he was, aware only of the immediacy of his agony. Then, as his eyes focused on the large iron collar that harnessed his hand to the wall, he returned to his senses. Underneath the rusting bar he saw the source of his discomfort—a patch of bright pink skin, laced with small rivulets of deep red, the product of the clash of metal and flesh made inevitable by the awkwardness of his position.

In an attempt to alleviate the pain, he shuffled on his back along the dirt-covered floor like an inchworm. By bringing his body closer to the wall he could now bend his arm and relieve his wound of the collar's direct pressure. But even with this maneuver, there still remained the constant throb of injured tissue.

His aching arm presented only one problem. From his position he could look up at the moss-covered walls whose sweaty moisture brought a damp chill to his own body. Below the rugged stone, littered across the floor of the abandoned reservoir, were pools of stagnant water, reeking of stench and harboring thousands of mosquitoes. There were the cramps in his legs, which were only relieved every few days when he and the other men were taken to the far end of the underground prison to deficate. Adding to this the brutality of the warders and the putrid gruel they were fed every evening, the discomfort of his wounded limb seemed minor.

It had been three weeks now that he had been confined to the Síyáh-Chál, four weeks since that rueful evening when he and his friends were caught trying to leave Tabriz. Now, as he looked around at those who shared his fortune, some sleeping from exhaustion, some squirming and moaning, others with blank looks on their faces, he mused at how ironic fate could be. He who had planned to turn himself in, only to be convinced by Mírzá Reza to flee, now found himself tasting the fruits of his original desire. His companion, whose only wish was to escape persecution, had been brutally murdered on the outskirts of Tabriz.

At first, everything had gone well. As planned, Mírzá Rahim and his comrades, about twenty in all, had arrived at the house a few minutes past midnight. Hasan and Reza were ready. The small party took little time negotiating its way through the back streets of Tabriz. But as they reached the city's edge, they were swooped upon by a band of horseman who darted out from behind a large clump of bushes along the roadside. In the ensuing melee nearly all of the Bábís were killed, including Reza, who fell to the blow of a sword amid hysterical shouts of "*Alláh-u Akbar!*"

For some reason unknown to him, Hasan's life had been spared. Clubbed into unconsciousness, he was taken to the same barracks where Amin had been remanded. Several days later, he was removed to Níyávarán from where he and fifty others were marched to the underground prison known as the "Black Pit."

The light of dawn trickled through the cracks of the damp overhead planks and down the cold, fungus-black walls. To this wall, pairs of men were chained. Hasan heard the soft voice of his neighbor. "Did you get any sleep?"

Hasan slowly rotated his body and turned his head to face Rahim. "As much as could be expected."

"And how is your arm?"

"Very sore. I think it is festering."

Rahim squinted downward and examined the wound as best he could. "You should say the Báb's healing prayer," he suggested. "Husayn-'Alí has been saying it daily."

Had he referred to anyone else, the young man would have scoffed at the suggestion. But the nobleman from Núr of whom Rahim spoke was unlike anyone Hasan had met. Hasan remembered him from Badasht, where his stirring speech had rallied the fractured community. But it was only on the march to Tehran, when Hasan had observed him at close quarters, that he had become aware of the depth of his personal power. While others, including those with the most devout and pious convictions, had at times lost their spirit during the gruelling ordeal, Husayn-'Alí had never wavered. Amid the heat, dirt, filth, and pain that marked that journey, amid the insults heaped upon them in nearly every village and hamlet through which they passed, he maintained an uncompromising serenity. When others fell, he was the first to rush to their side. Even the guards, who were ordered to have no mercy on their captives, came to treat him with respect. Thus, although Hasan had long since lost belief in such supplications, the fact that the advice was mentioned in association with this man caused him to answer his friend respectfully. "If I had his faith—"

"It is strange that you say that," said Rahim softly. "During our march here I had the occasion to speak similar words to him. It was not long after we had left Níyávarán. We were passing through a small village when an elderly woman ran out throwing rocks at us. My reaction was to curse her, and the guards tried to shove her away. But Husayn-'Alí told them to leave her alone—that they should not interfere with what she thought was a meritorious act in the eyes of God. Afterwards, I told him that I had never seen such faith. He answered that it was not a matter of faith, but of love."

It was several moments before Hasan replied. "Then perhaps my love is not strong enough," he said.

By now the rays of the rising sun had become solid lines of light, and the noises of the awakening city could be faintly heard in the distance. "Another day," murmured Hasan. How long they seemed when there was no escape from the solitary web of one's own being.

In the middle of his melancholic reflection, Hasan heard a melodious voice emanating from the long row of prisoners opposite him. Looking up to find the source of song, he found himself gazing at the very man about whom he and Rahim had been speaking. Moreover, as he listened to the well-formed words which poured out of Ḥusayn-'Alí's mouth, he realized that he was chanting the healing prayer.

As the verses continued to flow, Hasan stared at the figure before him. The face into which he looked was impossible to describe. Within its small sphere was housed an enigma. The piercing brown eyes seemed to read one's soul; power emanated from that noble brow. Yet, along with these signs were etched qualities of meekness and humility. Ever since Hasan had first seen the unconcealed power of that face on the road to Tehran, whenever he found himself looking into it, he became as one possessed, unable to look away.

After a time the chanting ceased. For several minutes Ḥusayn-'Alí closed his eyes in deep meditation. Then, ever so slowly, they began to open. Focusing on the object of their intent, his eyes suddenly sharpened. Immediately, Hasan felt the force of this man's gaze. It was like being shot with two hot arrows. Though he wanted to turn away, he no longer had control over his own will. The eyes were speaking to him, but in a language he could not understand. What was this man saying? What did he demand? Then it was over. The fiery orbs had set. Once again Ḥusayn-'Alí returned to the serene posture of meditation, leaving Hasan quivering in awe.

THREE DAYS PASSED. Although the experience was not repeated, Hasan could not forget the intensity of those few seconds. Were it not for the fact that another event entered the deepest regions of his emotional world, he would have been consumed by the haunting vision of the eyes of Ḥusayn-'Alí. Only one thing could have distracted him— the reintroduction of daily executions.

Upon arriving at the Síyáh-Chál, the Bábís had been subjected to the torment of having one of their companions removed each morning, never to return. While most of those selected to meet their end did so joyously—some even in a state of rapture—the anxiety such occasions aroused within Hasan was almost unbearable.

He was not afraid of the pain. What he feared, although he did not understand it, was his own fear—an ungrounded, irrational fear, subtly mingled with the ever-present stream of meaninglessness flowing through his being. When one morning the guard did not appear, a great relief had swept over him. No longer did the dawn bring with it the anguish of listening for footsteps approaching the cell door, or the trepidation of having to watch to see if the man in gray would turn in his direction.

But only two days ago, the morning following his visual confrontation with Ḥusayn-'Alí, the guard had abruptly reappeared. It was just before dawn, and the dark seemed to ebb slowly like a lifting fog. Hasan was always awake at this time. He heard the muffled shuffle of feet advancing down the corridor. Most of the men were asleep, but the rattle of the chain at the door quickly woke them all. The flashing exchange of glances indicated they shared a common interpretation.

When the door creaked open, Hasan felt his throat constrict with fear. While the hungry eyes that stood in the entryway scanned the room, the lump began to grow—until it became a fist, choking and suffocating him. Like the others, he had fixed his eyes on the man's feet, waiting to see in which direction they would move. Although it was mixed with twangs of guilt, when the feet finally moved in a direction away from him, the feeling of relief returned, relief of being granted another day of life, even in the Black Pit.

Now, once again Hasan apprehensively awaited the coming of the dawn. Only the pain in his arm, now almost constant, kept him in the present. Like rabbits surrounded by hungry snakes, the men around him twitched and fidgeted as the light grew.

Abruptly, his fears became concrete. In the distance the sound of boots could be heard. The scuffling cadence became louder. The men held their breath. The lump returned to Hasan's throat along with the choking sensation.

They all waited. Suddenly, the iron barrier that separated them from the outside world was moving. Soon after, the doorway was filled with the heavy figure of the warder. As usual, the visitor did not speak. His head, which protruded from his thick-collared coat like a barren tree stump, merely turned. His deep-socketed igneous eyes, resting under bushy unkempt eyebrows, adjusted to the dim light by spreading themselves as wide as possible.

From his far corner, Hasan concentrated on the guard with the force of his entire being. Any brief hesitation, any slight movement, might indicate that he had found his man. All of his senses were heightened; existence itself seemed to have become distilled into that one bitter moment.

One by one the prisoners felt themselves examined by the man's searching eyes. With each movement of those eyes, Hasan could feel the knot in his throat tighten. Over half of the men had now been viewed, and still the guard's head moved.

As the pressure mounted, Hasan looked away. But the intensity of the moment did not allow him to keep this posture. Again he glanced toward the iron door. Still the warder had not moved. He had never before taken so long . . . There was a pause. Like a clock that had stopped ticking, the jailer's head became still. The hunter had found his prey.

Hasan's eyes remained fixed on the warder's lower limbs. When would they move to reveal their secret? The answer came quickly. Deliberately, one foot after another, the heavy coated figure moved. After several steps, Hasan realized that the guard was coming in his direction. Hastily, he glanced at Rahim; his companion was absorbed in prayer. Should he whisper a warning of the approaching doom?

The sound of the warder's voice put an end to his speculation. "Hasan-i Bastami," he bellowed. "Hasan-i Bastami!" he repeated after a moment, in an agitated and noticeably louder tone.

"I am he," said Hasan, trying to remain composed.

The warder responded to the reply by removing a rusted iron rod from his pocket. Taking a few steps forward, he bent over and thrust it into the lock fastening the prisoner's arm-chain to the wall. Hearing the sound of the rotating key, the full impact of the situation struck Hasan. He was going to die. But all traces of fear had vanished. The fate he had eluded at Ṭabarsí and Níyávarán had finally raised its face to confront his. A new sense of acceptance swept over him; he was going to die a hero.

As the metal links surrounding the lock tightened, a piercing shock shot through Hasan's arm. He used all his mental strength not to cry out. Unconcerned with the pain he was inflicting, the warder grabbed the now unattached end of the chain and yanked it upward. On the other end, the iron collar dug into Hasan's arm, breaking the bloody scab and releasing a flow of water and pus. This time Hasan could not control his reaction. As he was lifted to his feet by the force of the guard's action, he let out a muted cry.

"Shut up, swine," yelled the warder.

Hasan did not answer. The pain in his arm completely absorbed him.

"Come on," the jailer shouted. Yanking the chain a second time, he started toward the iron door.

Hasan had not been on his feet for several days, and the first few steps made him stumble. The warder, however, did not slow his pace. Before they had gone much further, Hasan's legs buckled, causing him to fall with a thud directly before Ḥusayn-'Alí. While the guard scrambled to regain his balance, Hasan raised his head from the filthy floor and took a final look at the man whose mystery he could not unravel. The aura of serenity had not vanished, and their eyes made contact.

In that brief moment, a feeling Hasan had not known since Bada<u>sh</u>t welled up within him. He wanted to expose to this man his innermost self. Before he could respond, however, he was on his feet again, pulled from the ground like a leashed animal by the infuriated warder.

"Stay on your feet," the guard shouted. He accompanied his exhortation with a swift stroke to the side of the prisoner's head, a blow which caused Hasan to stagger and almost return to the ground. Only the jailer's weight at the end of the chain kept him erect.

Having vented his anger, the warder turned and started forward, and the two men gradually proceeded across the prison floor. More than once, Hasan's legs trembled and he thought he would surely collapse, but each time the warder rectified the situation by quickly sliding his hand up the chain to give support to the floundering inmate.

When they reached the door, the jailer stopped and fumbled with his keys. Keeping a firm hold on the chain, he swung the iron gate open. The break in the journey not only allowed Hasan to regain some of his strength; it gave him an opportunity to try for another glimpse of Ḥusayn-'Alí. But as he turned back toward the far corner from which he had come, the guard pulled him out into the corridor.

The narrow passageway led to a flight of stairs some fifty yards away. As Hasan trudged forward, through the haze of pain, which in periodic throbs set his entire arm aflame, the image of Ḥusayn-'Alí's cryptic smile remained with him—promising what? It was as if Hasan had been assured his place in paradise, but . . . Another excruciating pain in his arm cut his thought short, and he felt as if he were paralyzed. "Wait," he cried out.

"Don't stop now," yelled the warder. "You wouldn't want to be late." Again, he gave the chain a sharp tug.

By now the two men had reached the stairs at the end of the corridor. Somehow Hasan found the strength to begin the climb to the courtyard above. Ever so slowly, making sure that both feet were firmly established on each step before moving to the next, Hasan made his way up.

Angered by the slowness of their pace, the warder periodically turned around as if to pull Hasan along. But each time his irritation was checked by the realization that any such attempt might result in another fall. Time and again he begrudgingly waited for his prisoner to reach the next step before moving on.

When they were three-quarters of the way to the top, Hasan's eyes were cut by the sunlight streaming in from the doorway above them. It was the first unfiltered light he had seen for weeks. Its force caused him to cover his eyes with his free hand. Yet, the penetrating warmth gave him a rush of inner strength, which he boldly and unexpectedly exhibited by declaring to his captor: "Your prison is our mosque!"

The guard, his labored breathing revealing his fatigue, did not strike out at Hasan but kept moving relentlessly upward. Several minutes later, having reached the final step, he took one last stride and lurched out into the open air. The full impact of the sunlight now made itself felt. For the remainder of the trip across the sandy enclosure, Hasan was not only hounded by pain, he was virtually blinded as well.

Some fifty yards away, and at right angles to the underground opening from which the men had emerged, stood the prison headquarters. It was toward this small, shabby building that the warder escorted Hasan. Inside sat the local magistrate, an innocuous, clean-shaven little man whose gray uniform matched those of the prison warders.

193

Only the shiny buttons on his collar, which sat up like colored beetles on a decaying tree, gave any indication that he was a man of significance. His desk was littered with papers, through which he was busy rifling. Every few seconds, he seemed to find something of significance which he would put aside in a separate pile before nervously returning to the flurry of ink-stained correspondence. So engaged was he in this process that he did not hear the footsteps outside his half-open door announcing the arrival of the warder and his prisoner. Were it not for the sound of the jailer's voice requesting permission to enter, he might have allowed them to remain standing in the hallway indefinitely.

"Yes, yes, ah . . . enter," he stuttered.

The warder pushed open the door and walked into the room. Behind him Hasan shuffled in, still attached to the man by a yard of chain. Though he could now see, his eyes remained sensitive. He had all he could do just to keep them open.

When the men were positioned a few feet from the large wooden desk, the magistrate spoke. "You are Hasan-i Bastami?"

"Yes," answered Hasan, still squinting.

The magistrate began sorting through one of the large piles of paper in front of him.

He's looking for the warrant, thought Hasan. In a defiant, almost goading voice, he addressed the official. "You don't have to waste time for my sake. I am ready now. God has created me for this moment."

The magistrate ignored the comment and continued his search. After several seconds, he found what he was looking for and pulled a fresh-looking piece of paper from the pile. Two minutes later, he was still examining the document. Despite the constant throb in his arm, Hasan's mental state began to shift. "He's toying with me," he whispered.

"Shut up," cried the warder. With the intent of enforcing his command, he raised his hand menacingly. But before the warder could carry his thought any further, the magistrate thrust the paper down on his desk and ordered the man to unlock Hasan's arm chain. Caught completely by surprise, the guard stood dumbfounded. As a symbol of humiliation, all followers of the Báb were sent to their deaths with their chains on. Now that he was ordered to remove the iron manacle, he acted like a hunter who had been asked to remove his prey from the trap.

"Hurry up," insisted the magistrate.

"But . . ."

"Do as you are ordered!" yelled the magistrate, raising his voice for the first time.

The confused warder took the large iron key from his pocket and thrust it into the lock that restrained Hasan's wrist. Sharing the man's puzzlement, the prisoner watched as the heavy ring was loosened and then removed.

"You are free to leave," said the magistrate.

Hasan opened his now-adjusted eyes in wide disbelief. He wanted to say something, but the words would not come.

"This order has just come down from the ministry," continued the official. "Your brother is waiting for you outside. The yard sentry will see to it that you are escorted to the gate."

Both Hasan and the warder remained frozen, unable to grasp what they were hearing. While they stared at the magistrate, he returned to the task of sorting papers. After several seconds, the official became aware that his command was not being carried out. Papers in hand, he looked up at the two figures in front of him. "You can go, Bábí dog," he repeated, with a gesture of impatience. "You are free to go!"

Still in a state of shock, Hasan looked at the warder. Finally realizing that he was no longer under his power, he turned and fled from the room.

Chapter 21

HASAN PICKED UP one of the pebbles that lined the roadway leading to the caravanserai and tossed it, almost effortlessly, into a nearby pool. The impact of the stone on the water sent ripples racing across its surface. As he watched the ever-expanding rings, he could not help thinking how much his own life was like the pond before him. How many rocks had been thrown into his own existence, with the same effect? Sometimes it seemed that his life was not in his own hands. Like those scurrying waves, its speed and direction were determined for him. Why was he here now? What stroke of fate had brought Nematullah to the capital to seek his release? Even more incredibly, how had he been able to secure his freedom?

Yes, Nematullah had told him the story several times. In fact, the entire trip from the prison to the caravanserai had been spent talking about little else. He knew how, having met with an important official, and having explained that one son in the family had already been executed, Nematullah had pleaded with the man to come to his assistance. And how with the help of a handsome sum, that same official had arranged his release on the grounds of compassionate consideration. But this was not what Hasan meant. Why did these things happen? Nematullah's explanation was only a description of what had occurred. It did not touch the depths of his question.

Hasan threw another stone and continued on toward the old mosque. Seeing it from a distance, memories began to return. Like a man reading a story, his head filled with images of his meeting with the dervish. Then there was the quarrel with Nematullah, and his own silent departure which had initiated the journey that had led him to Bada<u>sh</u>t, Ṭabarsí, Tabriz. It all seemed strange, so far away.

Surprisingly, Nematullah had said nothing about the past. Once Hasan had overcome the shock of being released into the waiting arms of his brother, he had expected to hear his condemnation. Not once, however, during the trip to the caravanserai had his brother raised the issue. This silence had been maintained for the entire three months they had been together. Of course, Amin was mentioned, but only in a manner befitting the memory of lost loved ones. At first Hasan thought that Nematullah's subdued behavior was a result of the presence of their mother and sister, both of whom were now living at the caravanserai. Yet as the days wore on, he realized that a drastic change had come over his older brother, a change which he came to accept as the product of profound suffering.

By this time, Hasan had returned to the present. Entering the small garden that surrounded the mosque, his eyes suddenly filled with color. It was his mother who had insisted that the garden be rejuvenated. She had always been fond of flowers. Even now Hasan could remember the times in Shiraz when he and Amin would be scolded for picking the roses. Her voice shrill with emotion, and her hands waving in the air, she would run from the house. Reaching the small culprits, she would calm herself before slowly reciting a verse from Firdawsi:

> Roses are a gift of price
> Sent to us from Paradise.

More divine our nature grows
in the Eden of the rose.

It had been four years since Hasan had last seen his
mother. Now, like Nematullah, she seemed a different
person. The gaiety and spontaneity of her personality
seemed to have been drained away. She seldom laughed;
her eyes were always filled with a sorrowful, far-off look.
No doubt, this was why Nematullah had brought her to
the caravanserai. But the change in atmosphere had done
little for her spirit. In fact, only the spriteliness of his
younger sister, who was perhaps too young to feel the full
impact of Amin's loss, was reminiscent of the domestic
scene Hasan used to know.

Hasan sat down under a large fig tree, his mind lost in
thoughts of Nematullah and his mother. Slowly, yet inex-
orably, he returned to the subject which had governed his
consciousness since he had left the Síyáh-Chál. Why had
he been freed? He reached into the dirt, picked up another
rock, and sent it hurtling across the garden.

For the next few minutes Hasan sat still, allowing his
mind to remain in a state of limbo. Perhaps it was God's
way of . . . "No, I don't believe in God," he blurted out,
as if addressing someone. Yet Hasan realized that a man
who was sure of himself would not be tormented as he was.
It was only chance, he thought, trying to avert the question
that hovered in his mind, unstated. But he could not
escape. It was pursuing him, forcing him back into himself.

Could he believe? Though the thought made him feel
sick, it was a question he had to answer. For the next hour
he wrestled with it, examining his past with an intensity
he had not known since the night in Tabriz following

Amin's execution. He had resigned himself to meaning-lessness in the universe and had sought refuge in self-asser-tive action—purposeless energy. In the core of his being, God had died. Then, in the Síyáh-Chál, that dead God had once again begun to stir within him: somehow he had felt a new strength and was ready to die in faith. But with his release, the gap yawned open before him once more. His faith was gone, perhaps never to return.

Another hour passed. The time for his midday meal had come and gone, yet Hasan felt no hunger. His thought was riveted on a single image: a man standing on a cliff, peering across to another ledge with no means of getting there. He was at a standstill; his mind became quiet.

Out of the corner of his eye, Hasan noticed something moving. Glancing at the branch above him, he focused on a large brown spider spinning its web. Periodically, the small creature would fling itself from the security of its wooden base and dangle unaided in midair before attaching itself to the center of the ever-growing net. Sec-onds later, it would again cast itself confidently adrift, then slowly glide across the abyss to the next branch. For several minutes Hasan watched this process, his mind caught somewhere between thought and disinterested observation. Then a fantastic idea came into his head. What if there was no gap? Why did God have to be some-thing out there on another ledge? Why couldn't He be like the web, something spun from within? Hasan's excitement rose as he pondered this new possibility. On several occa-sions he had heard Amin speak about communion with God in the deepest recesses of one's being. At the time, he had not understood his brother. Perhaps this was because he had always been taught to think of God as *other,* omnipotent, beyond.

He pursued the implications of his new insight with the fervor of one possessed. Yes, God had to be related to one's inner awareness of truth. He was not a partner in a relationship: He *was* the relationship. Of course, this meant that in traditional terms he was commiting *shirk*—men had been executed for such pantheism. But it no longer mattered. In Tabriz he had thought out the absurd conclusions of the old God and rejected them. The old God was, after all, a concept. As he knew, conceptual idols were much harder to break than ones made of stone.

Hasan paused to gather up his ideas, afraid that somehow he would forget them. But the mania of the moment would not allow his mind to remain still. God was neither the judge of the world nor the cause of the world. That dualistic framework which had molded his previous concepts was inadequate. If any symbol was appropriate for God, it was creativity, not creator; justice, not judge. God could never be static, just as time could not be static. Men would never know God or agree on what He was. All they could know was that they didn't know; and this gave them their integrity as men.

Again Hasan paused, this time because a question had entered his head. Wasn't he saying that there was no God? Were these thoughts any different from the conclusions he had come to in Tabriz? Wasn't he doing exactly what he was accusing others of doing—juggling symbols? A reverberating *no* shook his being. In Tabriz he had smashed old idols, but had not replaced them with anything. He had negated not only images and symbols, but life itself. He had severed himself from that source which was not a separate reality, but the very essence of his own being.

But what of Sayyid-i Báb? Again his mind had switched directions. What did He mean when He claimed to be the

Qá'im? Was He alluding to some alien force imposing itself upon Him? "Impossible," Hasan finally muttered. God was not a puppet master. These were the interpretations of men—small-minded men who perceived the universe in terms that mirrored themselves. No, he could not accept that this was what the young sayyid had meant. Revelation was not a magical event. If anything, it had to be a catastrophic upheaval within Being itself—a confrontation with Truth, the Truth that lay dormant in every atom of the universe. Yes, the truth of revelation must have its secret in the divine depths of man. As such, it could not be static. The Báb was the Qá'im in the same way that he was Hasan-i Bastami: it was an integral part of His being, not a divine cloak issued from above. This he could believe.

Fatigued by his efforts, Hasan leaned back against the massive trunk and closed his eyes. Twenty minutes later, he was still in a semiconscious state. Slowly he gathered what strength he had left, rose to his feet, and like a man of twice his age made his way across the garden to the roadway. Though cool, crisp air now rushed against his face, he still felt a pervasive exhaustion. By the time he reached the gravel surface, his legs told him that he had to stop.

Wearily he sat down and looked around him. In front of him, perched atop a waist-high bush, sat a small bird basking in the late afternoon sun. Grayish-brown in color, it spasmodically fluttered its tiny wings as if preparing to fly into the pale sky. On the top of its head was a single dab of white which seemed a perfect compliment to its short yellow beak. The surrounding neck feathers had been recently preened. Those on its chest, though by no means perfect in form, were also well shaped. The bush to which its wiry, black claws were firmly attached sprouted thousands of deep green leaves, some the size of a large coin and others no bigger than the wandering eyes of its visitor. Not quite round, the shape of the bush resembled that of an overgrown melon—only a few precocious branches jutting out from the right side ruined its symmetry. Beneath both bird and bush lay the soft garden floor, a fine mixture of mineral and decaying vegetable matter harboring unseen creatures of the soil.

The bird flew away. Hasan knew that it was time for his own departure. Picking himself up, he went back to the house.

Chapter 22

NEMATULLAH ENTERED THE ROOM and addressed his younger brother. "I am leaving now, Hasan. I probably won't return until nightfall. There has been some trouble in the far part of the district. Mother is in the other room. Perhaps you can do something to cheer her up."

"I will do what I can," replied Hasan.

As Nematullah busied himself with preparations for his journey, Hasan observed his brother. He looks so much older, he thought—his hair now entirely gray and his skin so dry. And what is more, he doesn't even seem to care. His dyes and oils are no longer put to use.

"I hope your trip is successful, my brother," Hasan said.

"*Inshallah.* If God wills."

When Nematullah had gone, Hasan returned to the quiet of his book. For more than an hour he read from the poems of Attar and Rumi, trying to see through the poet's eyes his own state of mind. He had not forgotten his brother's request, he was waiting for the proper moment. After he had digested the mystic images of his favorite verse for a third time, he placed the volume down and rose to find his mother.

As it developed, he did not have to. His mother was already half way down the hallway. He rushed to her side and helped her to the large divan.

Hasan's mother was in her early fifties. A simple auburn pantaloon covered by a white brocade shawl made up her morning dress. But it was not the clothes that dominated her person. What would have struck any observer, and was the focal point of Hasan's attention, was her heavy demeanor. The little-cared-for hair, the puffy eyes, the drawn cheeks, all revealed her dejected spirit. Once a beautiful woman, she had become haggard and old.

"Don't fuss over me, Hasan," she snapped, as she sank into the huge pillows of the divan.

"Mother, I will call the servants for some sweet tea."

"How can you talk of tea and sugar? Do you think there is nothing serious in life?"

Hasan found his own spirits beginning to sink. It seemed that whenever he was around his mother he felt that way. It was as if she had a contagious disease. Only concentrated effort to maintain his newfound confidence kept him from falling into her quagmire. "It is a beautiful day," he declared.

His mother began to cry. He looked at her, but could feel little. "He was such a good boy," she sobbed. "Why did he listen to those followers of Satan?"

Hasan knew that nothing he could say would now suffice. His initial thought was to leave the room. It was the woman, however, who made the first move. "Leave me alone," she announced. Pushing herself to her feet, she started toward the door.

Instinctively, Hasan rose to help her.

"I am fine." She stared straight ahead, wiping the tears from her cheeks. Without any further discussion, she walked out of the room.

Though he was no longer in her presence, Hasan knew that he had to get away from the house. Once outside, he headed toward the caravanserai's outer grounds, hoping that he could recapture yesterday's insights. But the feeling of well-being was gone.

When he was a few yards from the entryway to the mosque, he glanced up. His eye caught sight of a small cloud of dust on the horizon. Must be visitors, he said to himself. I should wait and accompany them to the guest house.

Several minutes later, two men on horseback came into view. Hasan stood motionless at the side of the road, his ears pounding with the sounds of horses' hooves. What a lovely sight men on horseback present, he thought: man and beast become one.

In a matter of seconds the riders were upon him. Streams of sweat rolled down the horses' flanks, and a dirty froth covered their mouths. Over their heavy and rhythmic breathing, the rider closest to Hasan—a tall, broad-shoul-dered man with a dark complexion—addressed him. "My friend! Peace be upon you. We have heard that there is a caravanserai located on these grounds. We are in need of rest. Can you help us?"

Although Hasan had heard the man clearly, he did not respond. His attention was focused on the horseman's face, which he was sure he had seen somewhere before.

"Well?" The rider seemed impatient at Hasan's silence.

"Yes . . . yes, my friend," Hasan finally answered. "There is a caravanserai just down this path. It is owned by my brother. Follow me. I will take you to the guest quarters."

"Good," said the other rider, a smaller and older man whose pointed features were made softer by his full black beard.

"Will you ride?" asked the first man, indicating that he had room for Hasan behind him.

"The building is only a hundred yards from here," said Hasan. "Give your horses a rest."

The two riders dismounted. Taking their animals' reins in their hands, they accompanied him down the roadway. Although he wondered who they were and where they were going, Hasan did not speak to them. He was busy trying to think where he had seen the first man. There was something about his look that made Hasan certain that at some time in the past he had come into contact with him. But when and where? Then it struck him. Yes! At Ṭabarsí!

Quickly he glanced up at the man, who was discussing a matter of seeming import with his friend. There was no doubt about it. He was the lieutenant who had killed Ali.

Hasan's anger now rose. Here was the cowardly man who had slaughtered his comrade, the man upon whom he had personally sworn revenge. Impulsively, he reached into his robe and found the dagger he now always carried with him. Wrapping his hand tightly around the blade's leather handle, he hesitated. But the image of Ali falling to the ground bolstered his resolution. Pulling the weapon from its hiding place, he lunged toward the lieutenant.

Hasan had been too preoccupied with his own thoughts to notice that, for some time now, the second man had been watching his unusual behavior with suspicion. Consequently, although his target was directly in front of him, when Hasan made his move, the lieutenant's friend was able to push his comrade between the horses, causing Hasan's strike to miss its object. Instead of hitting the lieutenant, the dagger struck the companion a glancing blow on the shoulder. Although the blade broke the skin, it did not penetrate deeply. Moreover, the oblique angle at which the dagger made contact with the flesh caused the knife to fly from its owner's hand. Hasan found himself on the ground without his weapon.

Rapidly recovering from his miscalculation, Hasan lept to his feet in time to meet the onrushing aide. Instinctively throwing forth his closed right fist, he caught the man flush on the jaw, sending him sprawling unconscious to the ground. No sooner had his knuckles made contact with the bearded chin than he flung himself after the fallen weapon, beating the scrambling lieutenant to the dirt-covered handle by only an instant. Then, pouncing on the officer, he skillfully used his strength to roll him over, establishing within a matter of seconds a position of complete control. "You beast," he hissed, squeezing his knees into the side of the man's chest and clutching his neck with a free left hand.

The lieutenant looked up at the face above him. Broken lines of dust and dirt covered Hasan's skin, and beads of sweat moistened his eyebrows. These things, however, were not what the officer saw. It was Hasan's wild rage that engraved itself on the soldier's mind, making him aware that his life was about to be taken. He gargled forth a last, pleading question. "What are you doing? Are you crazy?"

Hasan continued to glare downward. Abruptly, he rasped: "I know who you are."

The lieutenant strained under the pressure of the hand on his throat.

"I was there—at Ṭabarsí—when you deceived my comrades and cut them down."

The lieutenant's expression changed. His eyes took on a faraway look. "Yes, I was there," he said. "And I regret it. But I cannot change the past. I have made my peace with God."

The sincerity with which the lieutenant spoke disarmed Hasan. In response he loosened his grip from the man's neck and shifted his weight slightly backward. Was it another trick?

Before he had time to answer his own question, the officer spoke again. "Only three days ago, my friend and I gave up our positions in the army. We have joined your ranks."

These words hit Hasan with a startling impact. He was without words; he did not know how to react. Moments earlier he had been prepared to lash out with all his fury to kill this man. Now he just sat there. Could it be? Is he genuine? Then why is he here? Perhaps he was sent to watch me? Yes, another deception!

Hasan leaned forward and voiced his suspicion. "How do I know you are telling the truth? Don't forget that I have already seen you break one oath, a lie that cost the lives of hundreds of men."

Slowly the lieutenant raised his head. "Do you know Ḥusayn-'Alí of Núr?" he asked.

The officer's second revelation was even more jolting than the first. Despite his amazement, Hasan found himself giving the man a straightforward reply. "Yes, I know him."

"We met five days ago," continued the lieutenant. "He had been released from the Síyáh-Chál in Tehran. I was part of the unit assigned to escort him and his family to Baghdad, the city to which he had been exiled. In some mysterious way, he seemed to know who I was. On the very afternoon we left the capital, he approached me and asked why I had plucked the rosebuds from God's new garden. Normally, I would have seen to it that he was punished for such insolence. Yet there was something about him that stopped me and so I merely bade him depart. For the rest of the day, his words haunted me.

I felt pathetic, cowardly. It was as if I wanted to cover my head without knowing where to hide. Finally, in desperation I went to see him and revealed all. I can still remember the awful feeling as I awaited his rebuke. To my surprise he merely looked up, and with a compassion-filled voice told me to forget the past. "It is finished," he said. "Never think of it again."

Hasan remained speechless. Though he wanted to ask the speaker a question, the lieutenant's words had baffled him into silence.

"At this point I was trembling with emotion," the soldier went on. "Tears had filled my eyes, and I had all I could do to stop myself from crying. I could not look at him for the shame I felt inside. He put his hand on my shoulder and told me to join him in Baghdad. The next day, that city became my own destination."

Hasan found it hard to believe what he was hearing, but nothing could have prepared him for the shock of his captive's next comment. With the groans of his slowly reviving companion reverberating in the background, the lieutenant calmly issued a command. "And now, in the name of justice, I expect you to do your duty." Throwing back his head, he exposed his pounding jugular.

The combination of the lieutenant's serene words and the sight of his violently outstretched neck sent a series of shock waves through Hasan's body. As if thunderstruck, his hair stood out from his body and his vision became blurry. Had the officer kept his eyes open, he would have thought that the crazed countenance above him confirmed that his wishes were about to be carried out.

Violence, however, was the furthest thing from Hasan's mind. He was completely absorbed in his inner turmoil— a discord that brought with it a loss of orientation. What was formerly the face of his enemy suddenly became transformed into the visage of his brother. No longer was he on the grounds of the caravanserai: he was in Tabriz, gazing at Amín—the serenity, the fearlessness. Then, instantaneously, he was inside the Síyáh-Chál, experiencing again his own strength in the face of death. Now he knew intuitively what he could not see then, and it came to him as a voice ringing in his ears: "Only he who masters both life and death is free from fear of any kind, for he is no longer capable of experiencing what fear is."

Again the scene changed. Now the officer before him was on his horse, cutting down Ali—only seconds later to become the prison guard dragging his victims to their morning executions . . . And then his own image, knife in hand.

A seemingly endless series of phantasms flew by him, their pattern fluctuating between life and death, good and evil. To Hasan, however, this distinction was no longer important. In his enraptured condition he felt the unity of existence which the day earlier he could only contemplate. Whereas then he had seen through the eyes of his mind that the great mystery called the universe was in actuality one organic whole, he now experienced the full impact of that revelation. Yesterday he had been to the bridge, but not crossed it. The landscape and its benign interplay had lured him, but not seized his soul. Yesterday the unity was a void: peaceful but static, harmonious but without vitality. Now, everything around him seemed transfigured. They were the same trees; it was the same sky—yet all were ablaze with the flame of life. Here was reality, a flowing passion that defied all reflection. "Thou too art divine," he muttered. "Thou too art divine."

Hearing Hasan's words, the lieutenant opened his eyes

in astonishment. Had he so desired, he could have easily thrown off his captor. Hasan's weight was no longer pressing forward, and the knife that he had so menacingly wielded just minutes before had fallen from his hand. But like a man under a spell, the officer made no attempt to move.

Meanwhile, though Hasan's hallucinations had ceased, the impact of the experience had not left him. Outwardly his body seemed suffused with a new energy while, within, he knew an inner peace that words could not describe. No longer did he feel a need to strive for understanding. It all seemed so simple. Independent of conscious purpose, some profound inner resource had taken over—one which was beyond his mind, even deeper than his soul. What it was, he did not know and had no desire to know. He could feel it, and that was enough.

These moments of calm, however, proved to be only the eye of the storm. Slowly, from deep within his being a wave of emotion, the likes of which he had never encountered, began to swell. Before he could grasp what was happening, it had become a raging torrent. Rapidly his eyes filled with tears. As the rivulets ran down his cheeks, he was engulfed by a tumultuous joy. Moments with Amin, the childhood warmth of his mother's tender embrace—these could not compare to it. In his heart he knew that he was being washed clean. All the anguish, all the guilt, all the despair, all those feelings still lingering in the nether regions of his soul were being exorcised. He was made new.

While the lieutenant still lay motionless, Hasan sprang up. Reaching for the knife, he drew it to his chest. Holding the weapon firmly in his right hand, he lightly placed its sharp steel edge on the fully stretched skin of his inner arm. With a quick motion of the wrist he sent the blade flashing across the soft flesh, leaving behind a thin white line which moments later became filled with blood.

When the blood had gathered into a small pool, Hasan turned his arm and watched while the drops fell to the ground. As the sand beneath him became increasingly stained, he knew that he would again have to be become a pupil. Yet unlike before, he was now sure who his Master would be: the man whose eyes and words had pierced his understanding, the man who had transformed the enemy at his feet and made him a vehicle for Hasan's own salvation.

Deliberately he held out his blood-smeared arm toward the lieutenant. The officer grasped his outstretched hand and pulled himself to his feet.

Face to face, the two men stared at one another, and then threw themselves into each other's arms. They wept together for several minutes, sobbing loudly. Slowly, Hasan raised his head, looking into the lieutenant's eyes. Slowly, deliberately, he kissed his beard, and then both cheeks. They embraced again, kissing on the mouth. Tomorrow they would be on the road to Baghdad.